ALSO BY S. YIZHAR

KHIRBET KHIZEH

KHIRBET KHIZEH

S. YIZHAR

TRANSLATED FROM THE HEBREW BY
NICHOLAS DE LANGE AND YAACOB DWECK

AFTERWORD BY DAVID SHULMAN

FARRAR, STRAUS AND GIROUX
NEW YORK

Farrar, Straus and Giroux
18 West 18th Street, New York 10011

Printed in the United States of America
English translation originally published in 2008 by Ibis Editions, Israel
English translation published in 2011 by Granta Books, Great Britain
Published in the United States by Farrar, Straus and Giroux
Published by arrangement with the Institute for the Translation of Hebrew Literature
First Farrar, Straus and Giroux edition, 2014

This volume reproduces the translation edited and published by Ibis Editions in 2008.

Library of Congress Control Number: 2014949321
Paperback ISBN: 978-0-374-53556-8

Designed by Assia Vilenkin, S & R Design, Jerusalem

Farrar, Straus and Giroux books may be purchased for educational, business, or
promotional use. For information on bulk purchases, please contact the Macmillan
Corporate and Premium Sales Department at 1-800-221-7945, extension 5442, or
write to specialmarkets@macmillan.com.

www.fsgbooks.com
www.twitter.com/fsgbooks • www.facebook.com/fsgbooks

11 13 15 17 19 20 18 16 14 12

Ibis Editions and the translators would like to thank Nitsa Ben-Ari, Isaac Zailer,
and Gideon Nevo for their generous help. Special thanks as well to the Maor
Foundation, Jerusalem and St. Louis.

KHIRBET KHIZEH

1

TRUE, IT ALL HAPPENED A LONG TIME AGO, but it has haunted me ever since. I sought to drown it out with the din of passing time, to diminish its value, to blunt its edge with the rush of daily life, and I even, occasionally, managed a sober shrug, managed to see that the whole thing had not been so bad after all, congratulating myself on my patience, which is, of course, the brother of true wisdom. But sometimes I would shake myself again, astonished at how easy it had been to be seduced, to be knowingly led astray and join the great general mass of liars—that mass compounded of crass ignorance, utilitarian indifference, and shameless self-interest—and exchange a single great truth for the cynical shrug of a hardened sinner. I saw that I could no longer hold back, and although I hadn't even made up my mind where it would end, it seemed to me that, in any case, instead of staying silent, I should, rather, start telling the story.

One option is to tell the story in order, beginning with one clear day, one clear winter's day, and describing in detail the departure and the journey, when the dirt paths were moistened by the earlier rain, and the cactus hedges surrounding the citrus groves were burned by the sun and moist, their feet, as of old, licked by flocks of dense damp dark-green nettles, as the noonday gradually advanced, a pleasant unhurried noonday, which moved on as usual and turned into a darkening twilight chill, when it was all over, finished, done.

Another and possibly better option, however, would be to begin differently, and to mention straight-away what had been the purpose of that entire day from the start, "operational order" number such and such, on such and such day of the month, in the margin of which, in the final section that was simply entitled "miscellaneous," it said, in a short line and a half, that although the mission must be executed decisively and precisely, whatever happened, "no violent outbursts or disorderly conduct"—it said—"would be permitted," which only indicated straightaway that there was something amiss, that anything was possible (and even planned and foreseen), and that one couldn't evaluate this straightforward final clause before returning to the opening and also scanning the noteworthy clause entitled "information," which immediately warned of the mounting danger of "infiltrators," "terrorist cells," and (in a wonderful turn of phrase) "operatives dispatched on hostile missions," but also the subsequent and even more noteworthy clause, which explicitly stated, "assemble the inhabitants of the area extending from point X (see attached map) to point Y (see same map)—load them onto transports, and convey them across our lines; blow up the stone houses, and burn the huts; detain the youths and the suspects, and clear the area of 'hostile forces,'" and so on and so forth— so that it was now obvious how many good and honest hopes were being invested in those who were being sent out to implement all this "burn-blow-up-imprison-load-convey," who would burn blow up imprison load and convey with such courtesy and with a restraint born of true culture, and this would be a sign of a wind of change, of decent upbringing, and, perhaps, even of the Jewish soul, the great Jewish soul.

And so it happened as we set out that clear splendid winter morning, cheerfully making our way, showered, well fed, and smartly turned out; and so, in the light breeze, we got out at a certain point close to a village that wasn't yet visible, and our company was dispatched to the flank, while some of the others were to cover the rear and the rest were to enter the village. And as usual there was nothing better than being in the flanking company. Which was moving off through unknown territory, setting out into the washed, cleansed existence of the fields, the pure pellucid air, among plantations partly plowed (from before the rage), and partly covered with weeds and grass (from the days of rage)—and it was so pleasant to slosh around on the muddy paths slippery with puddles and fresh mire, until your youth, albeit no longer so very youthful, burst forth with renewed vigor. Even carrying the "mission-case," which cut into your hand, might be transformed now and resemble nothing more than something or other that belonged to a group of people walking, let's say, to work or even, for example, a flock of chirping sparrowlike urchins. There we were sloshing, talking and chattering, joking and singing, not noisily, but cheerfully, and it was clear: there was to be no battle for us today, and if anyone happened to feel apprehensive—this had nothing to do with us, God help him, today we were going on an outing.

We reached a hill, where we crouched under a cactus hedge, and we were ready to eat something, when the man, one Moishe, the company commander, gathered us together, and briefed us about the situation, the lay of the land, and the objective. From which it transpired that the few houses on the lower slope of another hill were some Khirbet Khizeh or other, and all the surrounding crops and fields belonged to that village, whose abundant water, good soil, and celebrated husbandry had gained a reputation almost equal to that of its inhabitants, who were, they said, a band of ruffians, who gave succor to the enemy, and were ready for any mischief should the opportunity only arise; or, for example, should they happen to encounter any Jews you could be sure they would wipe them out, at once—such was their nature, and such were their ways. And when we fixed our sights upon those few houses on the flanks of that unobtrusive hill, from which we were separated by the plantations, the well-tended gardens, and a scattering of wells, we saw that this whole Khirbet Khizeh presented no problem, truly did not justify any further explanation. On the other hand, there were some trees, sycamores apparently, here and there, so venerable and tranquil that they seemed to be no longer part of the vegetation but of the inanimate realm. And then someone came back with some oranges, and we ate oranges.

Then we set off down the slimy gray furrows, which they hadn't had time to sow; we pushed open a big wooden gate set in a mud wall, and walked up a narrow path, between hedges of prickly pears spread with dung and chilly dampness, where deadnettles, fumarias, and flowerless fleshy plants twined in profusion and sprawled under their own damp drab weight, or hid coyly in the recesses of the cactus hedge, and we climbed up the next hill. From here the village lay spread out before us. We took our positions, set up the machine gun, and were ready to start. And when the one who was bent over his equipment listening and speaking into the wireless receiver in a ceremonial singsong informed us that there was still a wait until zero hour, we each sought and found a dry place to sit or stretch out and wait quietly for things to begin.

No one knows how to wait like soldiers. There is no time or place that soldiers are not waiting and waiting. Waiting in dug-in positions on the high ground, waiting for an attack, waiting to move on, waiting in a cease-fire; there is the ruthlessly long waiting, the nervous anxious waiting, and there is also the tedious waiting, that consumes and burns everything, without fire or smoke or purpose or anything. You find yourself a place, you lie down in it, and you wait. Where have we not lain down?

There was a time when we had just begun to go into the villages that had been conquered, when there was still something fastidious in us, so that we would rather stand or walk the entire day, anything rather than sit on that earth, which wasn't the soil of fields but a putrid patch of disgusting dirt, spat upon by generations that had cast their water and excrement and the dung of their cattle and camels upon it, those dirt plots around their hovels, touched by the stench of the refuse of wretched cramped human habitation. Everything was filthy, it was disgusting to pick anything up, and already in the afternoon of the same day we were all sprawled full length upon that very sickly loathsome pissed-upon ground, lying comfortably, in a hardened mood, bursting out every now and then into eye-dimming laughter.

Oh, those days in the dug-in positions. There was once this stocky guy, with a swarthy pockmarked face and a mop of woolly hair, who tried to amuse others by making faces, while performing appropriate contortions, dressed in a filthy undershirt, and for the thousandth time he pretended to be speaking into the wireless, transmitting repeatedly in a hoarse voice: "Hey babe, can you hear me, can you hear me? I'm on the hill, I'm on the hill, at the ruins, at the ruins, I need you, I'm waiting for you, babe, you hear me, over!" And everyone easily took the hint and responded with an uproarious outburst that, for fear of stopping, continued longer than it should have.

Carcasses of dogs stank and no one cared. Whole days in the desolate dust, in fetid boredom, in demoralizing danger, and in filth from which there was no escape. Lying and waiting for what would happen.

Or for anything. No one was virtuous enough now to powder himself against fleas. One knelt in a shaded hollow and lay down. And as the sun revolved, you cast a reproachful eye upon it and didn't move a limb—the sun could explode for all you cared and you wouldn't move. And when, finally, a pleasant sea breeze blew and slightly ruffled and stirred the screens of dusty filth that hung scorching and angry, a pleasant expectancy also flared up inside you, as though despite everything. Immediately the sorrowful wail dissolved within you and everyone started thinking about girls. Something about them all as they were, and something about one in particular, except that even before the wind had folded its wings, turbid powerfully rushing streams had confounded this small pleasure, until finally there was nothing left of it but a kind of foul miasma. Immediately there was a need for vengeance, breaking and smashing, at the very least trampling. They would beat the camel that was turning the creaking dripping waterwheel until their hands were raw, and kick the old Arab who had stayed behind to make sure the water was drawn, and who, out of eagerness to help and so as not to be useless, held the camel's halter and walked around with it, round and round for long hours, he and the camel together; they would shoot dozens of bullets at a terrified dog until it fell, and they'd get into a murderous argument with someone, and then slip back into boredom and idleness, and vile monotonous meals, biting, chewing, hurling the tin away, kicking it to hell, and adding similar outrages, and waiting for the thing to happen, to take place at once, for something or other to happen, and damn it!

When it was afternoon, which here was dusty, shimmering with glassy heat-haze in the distance, hinting at outlines of things that, apparently, were not from these parts, and would not reach you, boiling away with the thrill of a July day upon the spacious expanse of yellow-gray land, without a strip of shade, without any refuge, the diametrical opposite of dampness, when the dusty afternoon had boiled away in utter freedom, the hours grew longer and longer, desiccating, ending with great sadness, with a sort of nothingness that seethed up heavy and slippery, leveling everything, until everything was exactly the same, flattened and unimportant, and someone would not be able stop himself any longer and would leap up and with a shout rush down from the hill and attack someone standing by the well—from which the creaking wheel wrung intermittent spurts, while vicious hornets pounced eagerly upon every fallen drop—and scream repeatedly with uncontrollable fury:

"Jab the fucker in the backside! Get it moving! Get the bastard moving!"

That was what waiting had been like. But on this glorious winter morning, upon this luxuriant hill, when everything around was green and watered, it was nothing more than a picnic on a school outing, when all you had to do was be happy and celebrate the pleasant hours and then go home to your mom. We lay on our backs or on our bellies or on our sides, our legs spread out in every direction, our tongues wagging easily, chatting and chewing, everything that we had been ordered to do on this mission wasn't worth a thought, that village over there, the infiltrators within it, and whatever else the devil might put together here. We didn't owe anyone a thing, we didn't have to worry about a thing, and we didn't care about a thing.

Apart from all sorts of other things, all this might only be one further piece of evidence that this war had gone on long enough, as was commonly agreed, in fact too long, and the time had come, perhaps, for other children to come and continue the game, if it was impossible to do without it.

With the same ease and facility with which the prattle had sprung up previously out of the pleasantness of lying around and doing nothing it now died down quickly and stopped of its own accord—from what we might call, for short, aridity of the heart. We sprawled in silence. We knew so well who would say what, and what would be said by whom, and also how he would twist his lips when he said what he said, and even his manner of being silent, so that you'd rouse yourself and hurry to revive the chatter so as not to leave a silence, were it not for the laziness. Maybe that wasn't it, but as one lay idly about, thoughts would stealthily creep in, and we knew that when the thoughts came, troubles began; better not to start thinking. By the way, two or three of us had already, it turned out, really begun to nod off. Including one kid who had started singing a snatch of a tune under his breath for the third or fourth time, and had stopped because he didn't know any more or because that was all he wanted to say. Even the one who was amusing himself throwing small stones a short distance, and a moment before had begun to play the well-known game of throwing stones at his friends and feigning innocence, got bored with it, folded his hands under his head, sank back, and his gaze wandered up into the branches of the ancient jujube tree and the vast sky that swirled up directly from the summit of the green canopy and rose with a mighty rush to unfathomable heights (which he cared nothing about and paid no attention to), so much so that suddenly it was understood that it was all up with us. We would never succeed the way we once had. Once, not long ago. And something fundamentally different, and gloomy, had already been sown in our innermost being, and there was nothing to be done about it.

If this lying around continued, I feared that we would start to quarrel.

2

OUR WIRELESS OPERATOR, who had been granted a quarter-hour break, switched off his fizzling transmitter-receiver, came over to us, and immediately turned to Shmulik:

"Shmulik, you know what?"

Shmulik turned over on his side, looked at him with raised eyebrows, and uttered a single sentence: "Mmm."

"Whadaya say about those donkeys, and their incredible vitality," the operator said.

"What are you talking about?" said Shmulik.

"Yesterday I pumped three bullets into one and it didn't die."

"Where'd you hit it?"

"One here in the neck. Another here in the head just beneath the ear and the third next to the eye."

"And?"

"It didn't die, it just went on walking."

"Come off it. That's impossible."

"I swear! Yesterday, right by the camp. I'd just gone to check the equipment. I saw it wandering around by the fence. I blasted it right away."

"At what range?"

"Up close. No more than ten yards or so."

"And it didn't die?"

"No way! It just went on walking. Then it dropped."

"Aha!"

"When it got hit in the neck, it lifted its head up and looked. Blood was already spurting out of it like a faucet. So what does this donkey do, it goes on munching grass. I got it below the ear, and it gave a start but went on standing there, looking. That was too much already. I shot it in the eye at closer range and it took a few steps farther in the grass, and then, really slowly, lazily, it dropped and sprawled over. What incredible vitality!"

"A bullet from an English rifle would have finished it on the spot, no problem. It's the bones they have—like iron."

"But at such close range!"

"Once I shot a donkey from behind and it dropped right away. This great balloon came out of its behind, and it pushed its head into the sand and fell over."

"It's amazing," a third person joined in the conversation. "With a camel it's just one-two and it drops. It turns its head around and, bingo, it falls. So how come with a donkey it's different?"

The one who was singing from time to time under his breath, his turn came round yet again, and he started quietly intoning the only snatch of music he knew, and someone else joined him with a sonorous blast. Our Moishe, the company commander, turned his head toward him and said:

"Stop that screeching. Lie down and shut up." He raised himself on his elbow so he could accompany his words with a glare. In the process he also glanced at his watch and said:

"What are they doing over there, when are we going to start?"

"What are you complaining about?" somebody replied drowsily without opening his eyes.

"I'd have fixed things here completely differently," said Moishe, rising and sitting, and pointing around him with the first stalk that came to hand: "I'd have laid some mines for them."

No one objected. Moishe the company commander warmed to his theme:

"That would have been great. Look: if the village is over there and they can't escape to it, where will they run to? First of all over there. Right. There we plant some jumping mines. One Ayrab flies up in the air and ten lie down. Immediately the others change course and come running this way, straight toward us, right into the range of this machine gun, and they're totally done for!"

"That's right," the sleepy one sat up. "Well, why not?"

"I dunno. They've decided to turn vegetarian. They'll get them up in the hills and that's all. Tomorrow they'll be back again. The day after we'll kick them out again. Finally we'll cut a deal: three days they're here, three days they're in the hills, and we'll see who gets fed up with the game first."

"This here, this isn't a war, it's a children's game," the one who had been dozing declared, stretching himself out full length; he was a young guy with nice hair and a blond mustache, a red-and-white *keffiyeh* knotted casually around his neck; you could see at once that only a couple of months ago his mother would have told him off in no uncertain terms when he came home late.

"Whatever happened to the good old days?" said a skinny guy. Gaby, one of those who had grown up around here somewhere, freckles on his nose, with uncombed hair and an unwashed face, and a bit of snot always dangling down repeatedly being sniffed back until his fingers and the whole length of his sleeve came to the rescue, always tinkering with some bit of machinery (this time he was the machine gunner), waved dismissively as he spoke, like someone throwing some trifling thing over his shoulder. And what was he referring to except that only a month or two ago, after all, we were sprawled just like this in the shade of cactus hedges waiting to move off. And the silence then was a rather different silence, in case some sound gave us away, in case the fear escaped and shouted out and bound our hands and feet, in case the thing got out and word spread that no one could promise, however insincerely, that the luck which had thus far saved you would not let you down this time, and up to now it had just been playing around with you—a humiliating, shameful silence before the action, small devious ruses to deny it—how nice and pleasant it was to sit here and casually say: "Whatever happened to the good old days?" as if to say: "Oh, for the great days of yore."

Of course we didn't bother with different explanations. We didn't even start. We didn't hear what he said, just "What's the good of sitting around uselessly," something with which our explicit agreement was signaled by the way we all looked at our man Moishe, the only trouble being that he was still lying on his back, munching on a biscuit and squinting up at the bright sky, so our glances were wasted. Suddenly it was clear that nothing was pressing. It was also apparent that life would go on one way or another. Whoever got lucky lay on his back blissfully; as for the unlucky one, no one owed him anything. And what a lovely day it was. And this valley before us. Suddenly our minds turned to this valley, and we surveyed it contentedly, as one assesses a thoroughbred colt.

"How many dunams are there here?" said Gaby.

"Thousands," they answered him, "and thousands." And immediately we began generously estimating its dimensions, expertly and easily dealing with thousands and tens of thousands of dunams one way or the other, making expansive gestures all around. Already we were dredging up from our memories and sharing things about heavy soils, semiheavy soils, *nazzaz* and *salag* soils, drainage, irrigation, and what have you. Someone even posited that somewhere there was a marsh, and that in that marsh there were ducks, and you could hunt ducks, wring their necks, pluck them, and roast them on a spit, and with some coffee and a few girls we could have a sing-along and a good time. And below, divided with hedges into squares, some large and some small, dotted here and there with patches of dark vegetation, or with spherical green canopies, or with hills yellowed with a profusion of groundsel, and plowed fields here and there, the valley sprawled peacefully, there was no cause for shame and not a human soul to be seen in the land, and the song of the luxuriant land rustled in blue, yellow, brown, and green, and everything between them, warming itself in the after-rain sun, gazing in total silence toward the light and the gold, throbbing.

"The devil take them," said Gaby, "what beautiful places they have."

"Had," answered the operator. "It's already ours."

"Our boys," said Gaby, "for a place like this, we would fight like I don't know what, and they're running away, they don't even put up a fight!"

"Forget these Ayrabs—they're not even human," answered the operator.

"I'll tell you what," said Gaby, "you see how beautiful it is now when it's theirs—when we take over it's gonna be a thousand times better, trust me!"

"Wow! Our old-timers used to break their backs for any strip of land, and today we just walk in and take it!" said the operator, and returned to his receiver, brooding apparently and thinking about things, and snatches of things.

The sun grew hotter and the day strengthened its pleasant hold upon the valley. I don't know why a feeling of loneliness suddenly thickened in me. The right thing would be to leave all this now and go home. We were sick of missions, operations, and objectives. And all these stinking Arabs, sneaking back to eke out their miserable existence in their godforsaken villages—they were disgusting, infuriatingly disgusting—what did we have to do with them, what did our young, fleeting lives have to do with their flea-bitten desolate suffocating villages? If we still had to fight, we should fight and get it over with. If the fighting was over then we should go home. It was unbearable to be doing neither one nor the other. These empty, godforsaken villages were already getting on our nerves. Once villages were something you attacked and took by storm. Today they were nothing but gaping emptiness screaming out with a silence that was at once evil and sad.

These bare villages, the day was coming when they would begin to cry out. As you went through them, all of a sudden, without knowing where from, you found yourself silently followed by invisible eyes of walls, courtyards, and alleyways. Desolate abandoned silence. Your guts clenched. And suddenly, in the middle of the afternoon or at dusk the village that a moment ago was nothing more than a heap of wretched hovels, harsh orphaned silence, and heart-wrenching threnody, this large, sullen village, burst into a song of things whose soul had left them; a song of human deeds that had returned to their raw state and gone wild; a song that brought tidings of sudden crushing calamity that had frozen and remained like a kind of curse that would not pass the lips, and fear, God-in-Heaven, terrifying fear screamed from there, and flashed, here and there, like a flash of revenge, a summons to fight, the God-of-Vengeance has shown himself! . . . These bare villages . . . As though you were actually to blame for anything here? Massive shadows of things whose death yesterday was still unimaginable, intertwining, silencing, stooping and clinging, some kind of question that posed itself of its own accord, or a kind of aside, that must be said, something about something that was not this, like this but not it, that left an unpleasant sourness, like pity for a beggar or a revolting cripple, which merely irritated and pestered the soul, and the best thing to do was to rid oneself of it, assume a furious glance and fix it upon that very village, what was its name, the one in front of us, and to translate the glance into a out-and-out curse, which, at the end of the day, when all was said, was the only thing that would be heard, and with such manifest enjoyment that everyone who heard it would taste the flavor of his own individual enjoyment, because, as was well known, a good curse was always in demand.

3

THE ORDER TO START ARRIVED. Our company was to open fire on the bottom of the village and the tall houses visible to us, the covering company to our rear was to open fire in its own sector, and the third company was to climb up and establish its base at the top of the village and dominate it from there. Our machine gun opened with a few calm, seemingly innocuous rounds, as though at a rifle range. At first it rattled the windows of a plastered house (pale blue Arab plaster) with green shutters, then it beat a tattoo on a tall clay house, and immediately the fire fell along an open alley, then sprayed over the fences and walls and among trees that the sun was starting to bathe even inside their dense canopy. (And this time was so different from other times, when your machine gun opened fire and momentarily stilled the earlier fears, so as to give the signal for the other, fundamental fear to sally forth, that here-it-comes-for-real fear, after which everything was veiled in a drunken blur.)

We finished one belt and started another. No one responded. Our sprays of fire cut the air, which poured aside, parting in their wake with a sharp rustling sound, then dulled and returned to its silence; there was no way of telling if the fire had hit home. Our man Moishe picked up his binoculars to check what had happened.

"That's good," said Moishe. "We really startled them. Push it a bit to the right. At those houses. Good morning *ya jama'a*. *Yahud* have come for a visit in the village!" said Moishe with relish. "The Jews are here."

We were lying on our stomachs watching the scene with enjoyment, and getting more and more excited both by Gaby's hits and by Moishe's wisecracks, looking around to see if we couldn't find some gainful employment for ourselves as well.

Now we could also hear the shots of the covering company beyond. And then, there was fabulous "cross fire" as it's called. "That'll tickle their tummies, ha," someone said. All unawares I had a fleeting recollection of how it had been for us, at home, only a short time ago, and a long time, and a very long time, and even beyond the threshold of the distant twilight of youth, when there were sudden shots, shots from the border, shots from beyond the citrus groves, shots from the distant hills, shots in the night, or shots at dawn, and rumors, and the blackout, and something huge, serious, threatening, and worrisome, and running, and whispering, and strained listening, and shadowy figures setting out with rifles, figures at once strange and solemn, running down the road, excited voices and somebody insisting on silence, and at once, in the same association apparently, came a precise and certain image, how in that same white-and-blue plastered house with the green shutter somebody had stood up from what he was doing in sudden terror, how in the mud-brick house somebody had stopped eating, how somebody in the cluster of houses to the right had silenced whoever was speaking at the moment—shots!—feverish shivering, guts clenched, a mother frightened to death coming out to gather her children in almost-heart-stopping panic. The sudden hushed silence, the well-known "pray-God-it-isn't-us, dear God," how for an instant the prayer hung in space, a long, drawn out, ancient, mysterious instant, peering out here and there before it was determined. Inside every single heart and inside the heart of all as one the pounding of a primeval drumbeat that cried out: danger, danger, danger! And they wanted not to know, were forced to reconsider and quickly make a frantic decision, while the whistling of bullets decisively declared: it's started!

"It'd be a good idea now to lob over a few mortar shells," said Shmulik, in whom the spark of battle had been kindled and who was ready to set it on fire; you could see in his face that he could already hear the howl of the shell as it flew through the air and the dusty thunder of its explosion. Without wasting a word Moishe quelled this bellicose suggestion with a slight shake of the head and a raised eyebrow. But Shmulik wouldn't back down. He asked for the binoculars and took a look around, turning the focus screws this way and that.

"Can't see a thing there," he said. "It'll turn out in the end we're attacking an empty village."

"Gimme the binoculars," Moishe replied without a further word. And Shmulik folded his hands around his knees and looked among his friends to find someone more affable.

"Hey Gaby," Shmulik suddenly said leaning toward the operator who was bending over his equipment.

"Whadaya got?" Gaby said.

"Nothing. It's a pity Rivkele's not here."

"You miss her?"

"You bet."

And he stroked the air with his hand as though hastily caressing a pretty neck, over which a cascade of sweet-smelling hair tumbled, tickling and radiating warmth, and, picking up the packet with his filthy fingers, he shook it to extract a single cigarette through the little hole that had been torn at the top, and lit it pensively in a cloud of smoke.

"*Ahlan*," Shmulik suddenly called, as the cloud of smoke dissolved, "look over there, they're running away!" gesturing toward the cultivated plots near the hills, whose lower fringes were hemmed with orchards. With difficulty, because of the rugged terrain and the striated background of the hills, we made out, continuing the line of his outstretched finger, a few frantic figures disappearing into the bushes.

"They're running away already? So soon? Without a single shot?"

"You can be sure that the first ones to run away are the biggest bastards."

"I'll blast 'em," said Gaby. Even though the plan was actually to let them go, because the more they left of their own accord, the less trouble we would have when we went into the village, and it would reduce the dirty work of getting them out.

"They're running . . . not even a single shot, bastards! Get 'em!" said Shmulik, growing more and more excited.

So Gaby swiveled the machine gun and fired several rounds. Moishe looked through the binoculars and gave him the range. We were all focused on that empty plot of land beyond which on one side were the hills and on the other clumps of bushes that grew thicker the farther away they were. Another group of figures appeared.

Shadowy figures that moved in the open, and seemed to be in a hurry, but their haste was negated by the scale of the terrain; it was like the meaningless writhing of a worm.

"Get 'em," said Shmulik. "A little to the right."

"You missed," said Moishe from inside the binoculars. "Farther to the right and up a bit. Now! Fire!"

We were getting excited. The thrill of the hunt that lurks inside every man had taken firm hold of us.

"Over there, too," roared somebody, pointing to another field where, like ants, many figures were running, their jerky haste swallowed up by the larger field. I asked for the binoculars and saw them, group after group, or maybe family after family, or maybe bands of equivalent strength as they fled, four or five or six, or single individuals—women, too—easily recognizable by their white kerchiefs over their black robes, and their running, because they were exhausted and short of breath, apparently, slowed for a moment to a walking pace, and then growing faster and faster until it settled back into a heavy run, which contained not so much speed as a concentration of all strength and breath to prove that everything was being done so that there should be running, so that they might be saved from their fate. That instant a group of three was clearly seen racing up a hill.

"Right there," I roared pointing them out to Gaby. "Range twelve hundred, to the right of that solitary tree. You've got a good shot at them!" And at that instant I shuddered for some reason, and with my hands still pointing with drunken excitement toward the runaways I'd spotted I felt somebody was shouting something else inside me, like a wounded bird, and while I was still feeling startled by these two voices, Gaby emptied several rounds there, and Moishe said, "To hell with you! You don't know how to shoot at all!" Surprised, I felt some kind of relief, maybe like this: "Let him miss, oh, let him miss them!" I quickly looked around to make sure that no one had seen me in what felt like my moment of shame. Immediately and uncomfortably, I went back to scanning that ditch in the field and tracking the panic-stricken figures that were floundering and trying to get out of it, but the earth could not contain them, unless they managed to get beyond those hills, beyond the horizon.

"I got 'em," shouted Gaby.

"Like hell you did," sharp-eyed Shmulik contradicted him, "gimme the gun a sec. Moishe—tell him to gimme the gun!"

"Those ones over there I can hit with a rifle!" said someone, Aryeh, who dropped to his knees, carefully aimed his rifle, and deafened us with an unexpected bolt of thunder. Meanwhile he jumped up and fired again. And the hunt was on, in full cry. Until Moishe stood up and said:

"Stop with that noise. You're such heroes, you. You shoot like my granny. Enough already."

Then Aryeh said: "Sure, just give me the machine gun for a minute and you'll see!"

Shmulik said the same, and Gaby was furious. Shouting broke out and they called the whole world to witness. The angle of the sun in the sky, the zeroing of the equipment, the color of the hills, the vegetation of the fields, the fact that the target was moving, the estimate of the range, which was somewhere between twelve hundred and nine hundred, and they reminded each other, and jabbed fingers in the air, once upward and once straight ahead—mocking, denying, being professional, and with enthusiasm for the one great justice—as a result of which Aryeh knelt and lay down by the gun, and everyone got out of the way, grumbling and insisting on their opinions, and made room, and Moishe picked out with the binoculars a group of four men who had just at that moment reached the angle of the hills and stood out beautifully with their dark clothes.

"Come on, this is it," said Moishe, "five rounds and you'll get at least one of them," and put his binoculars to his eyes. And we too screwed up our eyes in anticipation of the first shot. And those four opposite, whose strength gave way at that very moment and who slowed their running into a heavy stooping walk, went down one after the other into the dip of a little wadi, and one by one they came out again, and when the last one emerged the first round rattled out and the four were seen falling. Then three of them stood up and started running and skittering toward the cover of the nearby bushes.

"One-nothing!" shouted Shmulik, bowing politely to Gaby.

At that moment the fourth one stood up and ran after his friends.

"*Istanna ya qdish*," said Gaby to Shmulik with a slight bow.

Then a second round rattled out, followed at once by the third. The four people in the distance all dropped. Someone inside me choked. Time stood still for a moment and everything was unimportant. We craned our necks to see better, to get a better view.

Moishe said nothing. Suddenly two of them got up and ran, and before we knew what had happened they had leapt into the bushes and vanished. Then another one got up and ran. And when the fourth one got up, the fourth round poured out, the man bent over for a moment, waited, then rose—a fifth round. He didn't run but he walked. Then apparently he decided to crawl. Suddenly he began to roll along and was swallowed up in the grass. There was no point in shooting anymore. The contest had been indecisive. The whole thing had become tainted and there was no more will left to fight. I felt that it was impossible for me not to say something so I said:

"Let them be—you won't hit them anyway . . . It's pointless. Too bad . . ." And my words choked, but nobody cared.

"To hell with them," said Aryeh laconically, standing up and shaking off the clods of earth and a few sticky crumbs.

We were rescued from our distress by the wireless operator, who said that they were sending a vehicle for us to go out and check the huts in the orange groves and the orchards, and then we'd enter the village.

4

WE WALKED SLOWLY in the muddy tracks of the jeep that revealed its acrobatic prowess by bouncing around on all fours in the ruts and mire, which after so many tranquil generations of bare feet and donkeys' hooves were compelled to bear silently two scars along their entire length, bleeding mud and silence. There were no more shots to be heard, apart from a stray volley here and there, like an afterthought. If you were here on your own, and stopped walking, and listened for a bit, you'd no doubt hear the earth quietly smacking its lips, drinking, sucking, and lapping up the water, and the remains of autumn melancholy, dry and fevered, warmed and spread soothingly like the soporific effect of suckling.

Finally, when the road straightened out and stopped winding and meandering, alternately exposed and sheltered by hedges of prickly pears and acacia and by twigs threaded through rusting barbed wire, and became simply a damp dirt path running down toward the valley, the jeep stopped, where the machine gun mounted on it could cover the whole road ahead while we got out and went into the huts and yards to check them. And even if there was, it seemed, nothing easier than to disregard it, simply to deny it, it mattered to me that it was beginning. I was impatient for the beginning of things that I imagined differently from everyone else. I was content with everything and hated starting to feel differently, and I didn't want to stand out from the others in any way. It always ended in disillusionment. The tiniest crack attracted attention, turned into a gaping hole and started to shout. I took hold of myself and forced myself to keep quiet.

The huts appeared to have been uninhabited for a very long time. A harvest of fear and a crop of evil rumors had reaped untimely haste and the writhing of a worm hurrying to meet its fate. We kicked in the wicket in the big wooden gate in the clay walls and entered a square courtyard with a hut on one flank and another hut on the other. Sometimes, when they had the means and the time was right, these people would erect a clay hut over the casing of the well house below, training a vine or two and making an arbor, and bringing some concrete blocks, which didn't need plastering, at least as long as their corners were so attractive; pepper bushes and autumn eggplants were rotting below in the grass and moldering near the water tap, and roses peeped out of the rampant weeds and climbed above them, and paths extended to some place inside the groves. Another kick and a casual glance into an abandoned home, and a storage room where the dust of crops coated cobwebs both tattered and greasy-looking. Walls that had been attentively decorated with whatever was at hand; a home lined with plaster and a molding painted blue and red; little ornaments that hung on the walls, testifying to a loving care whose foundations had now been eradicated; traces of female-wisdom-hath-builded-her-house, paying close attention to myriad details whose time now had passed; an order intelligible to someone and a disorder in which somebody at his convenience had found his way; remnants of pots and pans that had been collected in a haphazard fashion, as need arose, touched by very private joys and woes that a stranger could not understand; tatters that made sense to someone who was used to them—a way of life whose meaning was lost, diligence that had reached its negation, and a great, very deep muteness had settled upon the love, the bustle, the bother, the hopes, and the good and less-good times, so many unburied corpses.

But we were already tired of seeing things like this, we had no more interest in such things. One glance, a step or two were enough for the courtyard, the house, the well, the past and the present, and their attentive silence. And although there might be an abandoned pitchfork or a fine-looking hoe, or a good, and valuable, pipe wrench, momentarily enticing you to pick it up and weigh it in your hand, as one might in a market or a farmyard, and things that ought to be in their place, and even stirring an urge, incidentally, to take the motor from the well and the pipes, five inch, and the beams from above, and the bricks from below, and the wooden boards (we could always find a use for them in our yard) and send them home, there was such a tickling pleasure in getting such easy benefit, in getting rich quick, in picking up ownerless property and making it your own, and conquering it for yourself, and plans were already being made, right away, and it was already decided what was going to be done with almost all of these things at home, and how it would be done—except that we had been in so many villages already, and picked things up and thrown them away, taken them and destroyed them, and we were too used to it—so we picked up the fine-looking ownerless hoe, or pitchfork, and hurled it down to the ground, if possible aiming it at something that would shatter at once, so as to relieve it of the shame of not being of use—with real destruction, once and for all, putting an end to its silence.

On the other hand, when we moved on and arrived at the cultivated land near the village, there were clear signs that the yards and houses had been abandoned only a short time before. The mattresses were still laid out, the fire among the cooking-stones was still smoldering, one moment the chickens were pecking in the rubbish as usual and the next they were running away screeching as though they were about to be slaughtered. Dogs were sniffing suspiciously, half-approaching, half-barking. And the implements in the yard were still—it was clear—in active use. And silence had not yet settled except as a kind of wonderment and stupefaction, as though the outcome hadn't yet been determined, and it was still possible that things would be straightened out and restored to the way they had been before. In one yard a donkey was standing, with mattresses and colorful blankets piled on its back, falling on their sides and collapsing on the ground, because while they were being hastily loaded, the throb of fear, "They're-here-already!" had overcome the people, and they'd shouted: "To hell with it, just run!" And in the next-door courtyard, which contained a kitchen garden, with a well-tended patch of potatoes, the fine tilth of its soil and the bright green of the leaves calling to you and telling you to go straight home and do nothing but cultivate beautiful potatoes—in this next-door courtyard, two witless ewes were huddled in a panic near the corner of the fence (later I saw them again bleating on our truck), and the huge water jar was lying across the threshold, calmly dripping the last drops of its water in a puddle, half in the room and half out of it. Immediately after this yard there was a plowed field close by and beyond it the outskirts of the village.

We had just reached the track when a swaying camel came toward us piled high with objects and bedding, its rope halter tied to the saddle of a donkey in front of it, which was also laden with household effects, great sieves and piles of clothing; it was standing and chewing the grass beneath the acacia bushes with exaggerated enjoyment, plunging deeper in pursuit of their juiciness with total disdain for its rope-partner that was anxiously lifting its small head to the full extent of its neck, leaning it backward as far as possible, as if to avoid a collision, expelling diabolical gurgles and fearful grunts, emitting a stench of greasy camel sweat. At the sight of the jeep it tried to break free and run, but its halter, tied to the donkey's saddle, held it back; it tugged and shook it with mounting force, but the donkey paid no heed to this camelious panic, it didn't allow itself to be distracted and just went on feeding lustily. At once our Sha'ul jumped down and grunted at the camel with a grunt that would make any knee bend, and tapped it reassuringly on its upraised backward-straining neck with the barrel of his rifle, and the camel, caught by a language it understood, was gurgling and arguing and spewing bitter speech, and already intending to kneel on its forelegs, amidst anger and wailing and complaint—except that just then an Arab emerged from the thick hedge ahead of us and came toward us with outstretched arms.

"*Ya khawaja*," said the Arab, who had a short white beard, talking while he was still walking.

Immediately Sha'ul raised his rifle at him and shouted to us: "Look who's coming!"

"*Ya khawaja*," repeated the old man in the voice of one who has decided come-what-may, "*Allah ya'atik, ya khawaja*," God grant you favor, Sir . . .

"*Yallah!*" said Sha'ul, slipping a bullet into his rifle.

"*Ya khawaja*," wailed the old man, alternately spreading his hands and pointing to the camel, breathing heavily, from fear not from frailty. "The camel, *ya khawaja*, let us take the camel and go," and while he spoke he was already next to his beast, holding on to its girth with his wrinkled brown hand.

"What's he mumbling," said Sha'ul to Moishe, who was sitting in the back of the jeep. Immediately the jeep reversed and approached the camel in a single movement that so agitated the beast that it pulled the rope free from the donkey's saddle (the latter gave a momentary start, as the bundles fell off its back, and immediately returned to chewing the succulent grass in the recesses of the hedge with equanimity) and shook the old man from his place with a sudden blow; terrified, he turned toward the camel and said a single word to it, a word it deserved, and how, and then he turned and clung so hard to the saddle that he became part of it, staring in alarm at the jeep that was pressing right up against him.

"Who are you, what are you, where are you from, and what do you want?" All these questions were somehow bound up in the single word that Moishe spoke to him: "*Esh?*"—What?—in a singsong with a gesture of his thumb and two fingers.

"The camel, *ya khawaja*, the belongings, let us take them and we'll go away, may blessing come upon you, let us take the camel and go . . ."

"*Isma, ya khtiar!*" Moishe said to him—listen old man!

"*Hai na'am, ya khawaja, Allah ya'atik, ya khawaja.*" The old man, sensing a turn for the better, became submissive and yielding, hoping and praying and ready for anything.

"Choose for yourself," said Moishe. "Your life or the camel."

"*Khawaja*," said the old man in alarm.

"*Ya nafsak ya jamal*," Moishe insisted, drawing out his syllables and furrowing his brow: "Just be happy we're not killing you."

"*Khawaja*," the old man was close to tears, he placed his hand on his heart. "*Allah*," he tried to say. "*Bihyat Allah*, by the life of God," he suddenly swore, striking his gray-haired chest, it was evident that he lacked one single great compelling word that might explain. "We're going—going," the old man said. "We have nothing, we're leaving everything behind," he pointed to the ground all around or to a particular house, "only a few clothes and some bedding," his tongue ran fast, so as to compress a lot of explanation into a little time, and his hands spread, like a man before his god.

"*Yallah*," Moishe decreed, "*imshi yallah*—get going."

"All right," the old man said, "all right we're going," with a slight bow of submission that was close to a shudder, and took a few steps backward, "we're going, *ya khawaja*." He stopped again and tried to say something more.

Aryeh fired over his head. The man was emptied of his breath and his knees trembled. He turned and groped in the air after a moment with his hands and started trudging along again. We all, it seemed, were sharing a certain unease, or else various thoughts were stirring. But then Aryeh said:

"Let me, Moishe, best to let me finish him off here. What do you want with this scum? Let them learn once and for all that there's no fooling around with us."

"You sit here quietly," said Moishe.

Hearing the voices, the old man turned his head, thinking that doubts were awakening that might be an opportunity to be taken advantage of, and he swiveled toward us with his little skullcap on his head, his short white beard, and his striped caftan open on his white-haired chest, and as he turned he stretched out his hands and murmured, "*Ya khawaja.*"

"*Imshi*—go," barked Moishe in a voice not his own.

The old man went. When he reached the turn in the track he disappeared. For a moment there was a sense of relief.

"Did you ever see anything like it?" said Gaby, wiping his nose.

"I wouldn't have let him go like that . . . some nerve, even to come and ask," said Aryeh. "Imagine if he'd been a Jew and we'd been Arabs! . . . No way! They'd have slaughtered him just like that." You could see he had plenty more to say, but instead he uttered a single insult with a viper's hiss.

"What are we gonna do with this camel and the donkey?" I said.

"To hell with the camel and the donkey," said Moishe, and we moved on.

We were circling the village to the south and climbing the hill when suddenly to our right the valley appeared bathed in the early light of the wintry day that was, finally, clear, blue-gold, sweeping like a wild wind or like the ocean waves crashing on the shore, shedding upon it green-brown-yellow, splashes of joy and generosity, a patchwork of fields, pathways, and their course—a tapestry of peasant wisdom, the weave of generations. We went on.

"I'm telling you it's not okay," murmured Aryeh.

"What?" said Moishe.

"That we let that old man go."

"Enough with that old man," they replied.

"Enough, enough," grumbled Aryeh, "that's the way it always is with you, but I'm telling you it's not okay, and some day you'll remember what I said!"

When we stopped in the shade of a mighty thick-canopied sycamore, whose circumference wasn't round but jagged like a star with unequal points and whose fallen leaves were rotting beneath it, dappling the ground with small patches of damp, with little rings of light, and with a sweetish smell of decay, the village was already partly visible beneath us, courtyard upon courtyard, some of them stone-built but most of them with mud huts, an absorbent abyss of enormous silence in which both our voices and shots here and there and the occasional braying of a donkey, which was broken up into a series of shrieks, along with the crackling of our wireless, sank like little crumbs that were immediately swallowed without trace. We started to peel off our warm winter clothing and to arrange ourselves comfortably, while Moishe surveyed the valley in front of us through the binoculars, not to examine its beauty. We lit cigarettes, ate oranges, and murmured words about this and that. I still had a strong feeling of being a stranger here, of being totally out of place.

"They're running, they're running," said Moishe, "they've harnessed their carts, they've loaded their camels, and they're running."

"The scum!" said Shmulik. "They don't have the balls to fight."

"Oh yeah," said Yehuda, a young cock, who fancied himself the cock of the roost, and preened himself with his knowledge of farming techniques, of seed drills and disc plows and diesel oil, so self-confident that he didn't bother to pronounce his *r*'s but said them like *h*'s.

"It's cleah," Yehuda said, without a hint of speechifying, sticking out his lips and projecting his chin, "they have no staying powah!"

Suddenly we were startled by the loud sound of a shell, and a column of white smoke erupted confusedly from the bottom of the village (the silence immediately dulled the noise, but not the surprise). When we fixed our eyes on Moishe, he explained that the sappers had simply begun their work. In which case it was time for us to finish our task.

"That's all? What the hell—we haven't done anything today!" said Gaby, sniffling and releasing the machine gun.

Immediately a pair of mighty shells exploded in swift succession, looking like balloons that were inflated to enormous size with incredible speed and burst, as a world of resounding silence streamed back into the great crater that was opened up. But like water pouring into an ants' nest was the sound of the shells to those who were fleeing, and you could see them even without the binoculars, running around desperately, sounds could be heard in the distance and other sounds from the hitherto silent village, screams, frightened sounds, and several shots.

Now that we had settled so comfortably in the shade of the sycamore tree, Moishe reflected and decided that it would be better for us to pull back from this spot, and make our way to a small track bordered with half-eaten, heavily pruned jujubes whose surviving branches were strangely twisted and thrust into space with many thorns and few leaves. We reached the beginning of the track where we found a little trench dug across the way, with an abandoned position dug in its side, a discovery that aroused laughter and disparaging remarks about the naïveté, the military capabilities, and the entire idiotic existence of those who had made it. While we were still scoffing, we looked a little farther on, by the side of the wide road, along which apparently the fleeing villagers had passed, and beyond which on one side there was a vegetable garden hedged with heads of prickly pear stuck into soil mixed with rotting fruit, and on the other side, the deep gully of a wadi with grassy banks, and saw two strange figures sitting on its edge, like two owls on a branch, dark, huddled, a single piece, head and body.

One or two of us leapt toward them and immediately recoiled at the sight that struck our eyes: two very old women in blue dresses and black scarves were sprawled shapelessly, horribly withered monsters that emitted the stench of newly dug graves, something inhuman, sickeningly foul, their nacreous blue eyes in their blighted dried-out faces stared straight ahead, either silenced by fear or in a senseless stupor. They had, apparently, been dragged here by their families together with cushions, baskets, and household objects; and here, in sudden panic or alarm, they had fallen, or been abandoned, and here they remained, exposed to the sun like moles in the midday, like a terrible deformity that had always been hidden indoors and had suddenly been exposed in all its horror, and here it was before us. What could you do with them but spit in disgust, and gag, and not look, and run from here—the horror! The horror!

"Yeah, yeah, I'm telling you!" said Shmulik with a grimace of revulsion.

"They're gonna die," said some guy named Shlomo.

"The devil take them!" said Aryeh.

"Scary!" said Shlomo.

"I would do them a favor and finish them off with a bullet to the head," said Aryeh.

"They're gonna die, look, they can't live," repeated Shlomo.

And without looking back we went on our way up the track to the left.

5

NOW THAT WE WERE GOING DOWN the slope again into
the body of the village along one of the lanes, wondering
if it was wide enough for the jeep to pass through,
and prepared for any kind of surprise that might come
our way, as the stillness of the village closed in around
the last house in the row, and the houses, still pent up
within the walls of their courtyards, apparently breathed
as they always had, only with a new astonishment, with
the same woven tapestry of generations line by line and
thread by thread, with an abundance of fine detail, the
reason for each one of which may have been forgotten
long ago and dissolved into the general appearance of
a structure fixed in its form, like the bustle of ants to
raise up something, grain upon grain, which, the larger
and more complete it grew, the more shamefully its
lack of purpose was laid bare, gradually exposed, and
the disgrace of its end, weeping for oblivion because of
what had happened to it: instantly its condemnation
was decreed, and very soon, here and there, the first
curls of smoke would hesitantly rise, accompanied by
curses because everything here was so wet and nothing
would catch fire.

Afterward another mighty shell resounded, and immediately the howling began. At first it seemed as though the cries were quickly stifled and placated as soon as they saw that no one was being killed; but the howling, a shrill, high-pitched, rebellious, spine-chilling scream of refusal, went on still, and there was no escape from the sound of it, you couldn't free yourself for anything else, impatiently you shrugged your shoulders and looked at your comrades and wanted to go farther, but it was no longer like the shriek of a frightened caught chicken, but like the roar of a tigress whose pain only enrages her, increasing her malicious power, like the roar of a convicted criminal being led out to execution, who hates and resists his executioners, a roar that is a defensive weapon, a roar whose meaning is I-will-not-move, I-will-not-give, I'd-rather-die-than-let-you-touch, until even the stones began to roar, a terrible roaring that gathered force with short breaks of snatched breath, and then it was even possible to distinguish words, but they were incomprehensible.

"What are they screaming about over there like that, what is it?" Our wireless operator couldn't contain himself.

"It's as if the devil has gotten into her," Shlomo said sourly, screwing up his eyes as though someone were scraping metal near his ear. Something grim passed through the village. A cow began to bellow desperately, confusedly, in waves of stupor, as though only by bellowing forth could she find a grip in a world that had been shaken out of orbit.

We had a sudden sense of foreboding as though we were about to be attacked, the alien walls were closing in on us, encompassing us with solemn malicious whispering, suddenly we seemed cut off, devoid of hope, no one knew whence the blow might suddenly fall—unless there were no other—and we ourselves here were it, in our image and likeness. We reached a crossing of alleyways. We got out to search the nearby houses. Everything was empty. The emptiness of sudden catastrophe. Uneasy boredom began to gnaw at us. The terrible screaming did not stop but turned into a wail of complaint rising fitfully, a hoarse wailing that had already become enfeebled, that was no longer a sharp scream, now that it had become clear that everything was finished, lost, nothing would help, nothing would be changed.

Suddenly a man emerged from the entrance of one of the sinister mud walls in the silence behind us. He seemed to have imagined that we had already moved on some way, and, startled to see us, he began to run up the road.

"Stand still, dog," screeched Gaby and fired off a round above his head.

The man leapt behind a stone that was standing next to the wall and lay flat behind it, retracting his head as far as the narrow space permitted.

"Stand up!" Gaby said. "Stand up I said."

He did not resist but stood up at once. He was in a terrible panic. Gaby carefully pointed the gun at him and said to us, "Looks like filth!" And immediately he pressed the trigger and let loose a "singleton" that passed within a hair's breadth of his head. The man spun round, spread out his hands and froze like that with his neck tucked into his shoulders.

"*Ta'al, jaiy*," Gaby said to him, "come here."

The man tried to move, and discovered that there was no connection between his legs and his body. Finally his legs uprooted of their own accord, while his body was still. His face was drained of blood, not to pallor, but to a revolting greenish yellow. Finally he somehow swallowed his saliva and spreading his hands out again he tried to smile submissively, the smile of a woeful mask, or to say something, but couldn't manage to utter a sound or even the semblance of a sound.

"What are you doing here?" Gaby interrogated him.

The man tried to smile again with no greater success than before.

"Looks like filth," Gaby repeated, pointing to him with his thumb. The man had a gray toothbrush mustache, and he repeatedly licked his lips. As though all his existence was concentrated in that licking. He placed his hands in front of his chest and described little circles of perplexity and explanation, without finding any firm ground for his soul between what there was before-this-very-moment and what was happening at-this-very-moment, and so he stood before us with the ground slipping away from beneath him, as the earth revolved.

"What's he wandering around here for? People wandering around under your feet always means trouble."

"He just didn't manage to get away in time," said Shlomo, uneasily looking around and searching for something.

"Why didn't he run away? No, no. There's something else here. I know his type. All this stuff he's doing to you, he's just hamming it up, playacting!"

"They've told him all sorts of stories about us, apparently, he's dying of fear! Ask him, Gaby, ask him what's up."

At this, Moishe intervened to point out that there was someone else who would ask the questions and that we should leave him alone, and move on if we ever wanted to finish, then, turning to the Arab, he pointed to the jeep, and to remove any possibility of doubt from his mind he pushed him into it with a wave of his hand so that the man was forced against the side and held on to it and folded the upper half of his body on board, while his knees on the hem of his caftan and his sandals remained dangling outside, and struggled in contortions that were ridiculous yet sad. They grabbed hold of him and rolled him on board like a sack, and when the man stood up it turned out that these violent movements had woken him from his stupor and he had finally found his tongue. Turning toward Gaby, whom he saw as our leader, he said with a despairing smile:

"I'll tell you everything, *ya sidi*. I'll tell you everything." But then he was seized with a spasm of nausea and began vomiting all around, as we leapt sideways in disgust.

"Scum!" Gaby shouted. "There's something wrong with this guy!"

"It's fear," Shmulik explained. "He's mucking everything up."

The Arab on the jeep was crouched over, still trying to cover the torment of his guts with a blank, meaningless smile of apology, as he wiped himself with the corner of his robe, groaning, smiling, and stifling hiccups, rumblings, and throbbings, and he was untouchable on account of his filth, an abomination with his vomit, fear, and smile, with some wrong that might have been done to him with his look of a respectable citizen who'd ended up in the gutter—we threw him some sack that came to hand and with exaggerated attention he set to work, using it for every purpose: to dry, to clean, and to wipe, trying all the while to calm down, to think clearly, to take control, to recover his composure, except that his trembling hands let him down. Finally he thought that he had finished and he turned toward us apparently with a word of commendation, except that a sudden shell jolted him, and his face changed for a moment, but at once he smiled sevenfold, a clasping, intertwining smile, the smile of an idiot.

"Maybe he's sick," someone said.

"What do you mean sick?" said Gaby. "He's healthy as an ox, he's playacting that's all."

"They don't even have blood in their veins, these Ayrabs," said Aryeh pensively. "To abandon a village just like that! Man! If that was me instead of him, you'd find me here with a rifle in my hand. For God's sake! I swear! . . . A great big village like this, and not even three real men. They see Jews and wet their pants. One jeep—what are we here, just a jeep and a few men, and we take a whole village. Only the devil can understand them!" he said, speaking words to this effect and other such things.

In the meantime, while Aryeh was ruminating thus, we descended and moved farther on, peering into the abandoned courtyards, calling out and announcing anything that had the status of a "find," chickens and runaway rabbits, pouring out some diesel oil that was on hand in a jerry can in the jeep, igniting a heap of straw or a wooden gate or a low thatched roof and waiting to see how it caught fire, and how its verve dimmed as the fuel ran out, kicking something here and there in case something more worthwhile was hidden underneath it, taking care and warning each other not to go inside for fear of fleas, brazenly slicing a cross-section through the life of houses, yards, and people, caught in mid-movement, leaving only a fossilized gesture that from now on would gradually wear down, silenced in the dust of time.

In a courtyard below we found two women who, as soon as they saw us, began to wail and cry, apparently trying to say something that couldn't be understood, both because one's complaint interrupted the other's and because the sight of their tears and awful grimaces, like a crying child's, elicited more ridicule than sympathy, and also because, despite everything, we were embarrassed at being in the presence of crying women, until finally Yehuda pointed to the doorway while his other hand gesticulated at them as if he were shooing away a flock of chickens, and he plied his tongue: *Yallah, yallah*—meaning: shut up and get on with it. And indeed the two immediately emerged wiping their eyes with a corner of their large white headscarves, sobbing in silent obedience.

Then in the next courtyard, on a stone beside a house, we found an old man who seemed to be waiting for our arrival and rose up to greet us, and began to pester us with the whole ceremony of greetings and blessings, and even tried to kiss the hand of our wireless operator (whose strange equipment lent him an air of importance), but he withdrew it angrily: get out of my way, you too! And immediately that white-turbaned yellow-sashed man began to lecture to us about how there weren't any young people left in the village, only old men, women, and children, and how he'd tried to persuade the ones who had fled that morning not to go, because the Jews didn't do bad things, because the Jews were not like the English, God curse their fathers, nor like those dogs, the Egyptians, etc., etc., clinging and speaking to anyone who seemed to be listening or who might listen, and finally someone pushed him in the middle of his torrent and said to him brusquely that he should go over there and shut up.

By the time we reached a little square down below, there were already seven or eight people from the village walking ahead of us, including a cripple who hobbled along on his crutch. They walked along without turning toward each other, they didn't say a word, they didn't look at one another. And so, without ever intending to be, we became a silent, sullen procession, a miniature demonstration in those desolate streets. All this began to weigh on us. And we needed to get rid of them, to stretch ourselves out somewhere and start thinking a bit about other things, and also to get some rest. The winding alley, the walls of the courtyards plastered with mud mixed with straw, topped with thistle stems laid across in a ragged pattern, wafting a last scent of summer (ah, that distant summer), the smell of the sodden village, the sound of silent desolation, seemed alien, oppressive, and superfluous. And our anger was still mounting when we reached that little square below, where two guys from another company were standing guard over their own little crowd that they had gathered in their own sweep.

"How many pieces do you have?" asked one of them, preening himself on the word *pieces*, and happy to appear like a big bad bandit.

"We have these," Yehuda said without looking at them but with something of a nod of the head, gesturing with a box of matches in their direction as he lit a cigarette.

"Look how many of them there are!" said the young guy. "If they only wanted to, they could've finished us off just by spitting at us. And look at the way they're standing."

The little crowd that was huddled there near the wall, men and women separate, was silent like a basket of freshly caught fish, still redolent of the sea. They looked at us in a kind of paralysis of despair, and yet with that same eighth-part of curiosity that bubbled up from fear, shame, despair, destruction, and the suddenness of a disaster that had just occurred. They seemed to imagine that now enigmas would be clarified to them and they could expect something special to happen.

Meanwhile our Moishe told the two boys to take this whole expectant crowd and convey them to the concentration point, and pass on the message that we were going to check out a few more places before we joined them, and he sent the jeep with them too. Immediately the boys started shouting and waving their hands and their rifles like gauchos in the pampas, ready to suppress and quell any trouble, but all the prisoners got going as soon as they heard the first cry, in an orderly, compact, obedient crowd without any protest, and all the hullabaloo that the boys made amounted to no more than pure heroics. Then one of the two took away somebody's stick, a stick with a round carved handle, and at once he shouldered his rifle, seized the confiscated stick and waved it around, pushing now one and now the other, knocking on every door, banging on every gate, hobbling along and leaning ostentatiously on the stick with a broad grin on his face. Then the jeep left, and then they turned in the winding lane and all went toward their fate.

6

WE SET OFF DOWN A TWISTING LANE, and as we snaked our way along it the village came to an end and there opened up before us a patch of grassy land fringed around with a few tamarisks, beyond which was the hedge of a plowed field. In the autumn, it seemed, the place had been a threshing floor, the lush after-growth of which now waved to and fro abundantly and evenly, as though no foot had trodden across it; moist down glistened on the slightly hairy leaves, washing the gentle sunlight that turned this whole space into a puddle of bright green fluttering with shallow sleepy breaths. We were so enchanted by the sight of this grassy plot that we didn't pay attention at first to a colt that stood in the far corner, completing the tranquillity of the picture, as it munched lazily on the luxuriant vegetation before it.

"What a beautiful colt, look!" said Shmulik, pointing to the roan foal, which raised its head quizzically and flicked its tail this way and that, raising a rear fetlock and kicking slightly as though brushing away some flies.

"He *is* a beauty," said Gaby, "he's gorgeous!"

"It's like another world here!" said Shmulik.

"And he's not even tied up," said Gaby. "He'll run away if we get close to him."

"He won't run away, he must be used to people," said Shmulik.

They advanced toward the colt step by step. Meanwhile the rest of us knelt in the shade of the wall and eyed them without saying anything. Shmulik bent down and plucked a handful of barley so as to tempt the creature, if not with the quality of the food, which was available in abundance all around, then by the style of his presentation, his attentiveness embellished with chirping sounds, paying no regard to how all the while his heavy boots were befouling the patch of green and leaving behind him a dirty furrow that revealed the mud.

"Come on, there, come on, there!" Shmulik entreated.

The foal whinnied with joy, stamping its front hooves in the direction of its new playmate, and gave some little leaps which revealed that its forelegs had been hobbled. At each caressing touch its skin rippled nervously, either from pleasure or revulsion, and it sniffed with moist nostrils that were black on the inside and adorned with a ring of white on the outside, its lips quivering over the barley in Shmulik's hand. Shmulik patted its neck and stroked its mane.

"Good boy, good boy," he sang obsequiously.

Meanwhile Gaby arrived, cutting his own dirty furrow in the field, slapped the colt's hindquarters and said: "This here, this is what I would like to take back with me." And then retreating a little way, he picked some grass and put it in his own mouth, chewed thoughtfully and mumbled: "I'd raise him to be a great horse."

"Say whatever you want about them," said Shmulik, "but they sure have horses, I'm telling ya!"

The colt, apparently drunk on flattery, decided to show off to us with a little dance in the dust, but as soon as it started prancing it got caught up in its hobble, something which soured its temper, and it made strange leaps, throwing its tail up and extending its neck as though trying to free itself from something, and showing the whites of its eyes.

"We've got to get those off him!" Shmulik said, stepping backward in alarm at the sight of the leaps.

"You'd better not touch him, or you'll get a kick," Gaby said, suiting action to words and withdrawing to a safe distance.

"What wildness, what a rebel!" Shmulik marveled. "Let's get his ropes off him."

"You'd better get back," said Gaby.

"That's enough now, that's enough," Shmulik chanted to the colt. And he tried to pacify it from a distance with a handful of grass. This time the colt didn't wait for the gift but danced a rebellious rope-dance with mounting anger, flailing ineffectively, its movements restrained by the hobble, all tangled up in itself, made frantic by the power of movements that had no range whatsoever.

"He'll break a leg!" shouted Gaby.

"We've gotta untie it for him," Shmulik answered. "It can't go on like this."

"He'll break a leg," Gaby shouted again.

Boldly Shmulik approached, one hand extending the peace offering of grass and the other reaching out with the intention of stroking and gradually calming the colt; he chirped pacifically but at the same time maintained a kind of half-turn in readiness to leap backward. The colt stood still. Its neck was stretched out, its head forced downward ready to butt, its back arched like a bow, its tail flicked up, tense, its four legs set at an angle so that its fetlocks were close together and almost in the same spot, like a grasshopper about to leap, or a drawn bow before the arrow is released. It paused in this pose for a short while, steely, lithe, seething with restrained power that might burst forth at any moment with uncontrolled desire, with liberating joy, and the breath of distant places and wide-open spaces. Then it straightened out all at once and raised its neck while its head, with tiny ears pricked up, tilted slightly to one side, as though sniffing at the wind, all attention. At once it relaxed its muscles. With a mischievous movement it turned gracefully to face Shmulik and extended its baby-like lips toward the grass.

Triumphantly Shmulik approached the colt, patting its silky neck and quivering belly, its reddish gazelle-like hocks, and speaking soft, soothing words of affection.

"Good boy, good boy. There, there. That's good," Shmulik said. And immediately he knelt down and drew his knife to cut through the hobble on the animal's forelegs. He thrust his head and most of his body between the four legs of the attentive colt.

"You'd better not stick your head down there," said Gaby excitedly, and took one step forward. At that very moment the horse started and gave a great leap, spreading its tail like a peacock, its mane waving wildly. It gave another leap forward and with head extended broke into a mighty gallop, jumped the low hedge (with a bit of rope dangling from one of its forelegs), and appeared one last time at the end of the plowed field before vanishing from sight.

With gaping mouth and dim eyes Shmulik got up and turned toward us, holding the knife, amazed and stunned, the words wrenched from his mouth: "Wow . . . did you see that! . . . I'm telling tell you!"

Meanwhile Gaby opened his mouth wide and burst out laughing, laughing and coughing, laughing and slapping his knees, laughing and looking backward at us and forward toward Shmulik, as he tried to say something that was lost in the howls of his laughter, which infected us all, until there was a general uproar, screeching, mocking, that extracted all sorts of things that we hadn't said all day and brought them out into the open, freely, publicly, all at once, and then Aryeh said, with a fleeting hint of a smile (because he had never done more than smile in his life) to the poor guy: "There goes your fifty pounds!"

"Fuck your fifty pounds," muttered Shmulik, reaching for his knife and returning it to its sheath, and turning away from us as he looked into the distance toward what had disappeared, while the field still throbbed with a wonderful echo of thundering hooves.

However, it was now clear that we had wasted too much time here. We got up unwillingly and returned to the alleys of the village. We checked the houses casually. We peered dutifully here and there, interpreting the sense of gloom that had fallen upon us as though it were merely a sign that it was lunchtime. Shmulik dejectedly trudged along in the rear, and when we tried to hurry him along he responded evasively and said to us, "What do you know about it! You don't see a horse like that every day!" and returned to his sad thoughts. In the meantime we also picked up a few Arabs, whom we gathered into a group and sent on ahead of us without paying any attention to how they looked or what they had to say or needed, nor to the occasional fit of weeping, and even the one who had for some reason prepared an impromptu white flag and approached us waving it and murmuring a formal address, as if he were the village headman and was holding the keys of surrender, even he aroused in us only feelings of boredom, inexplicable anger that gradually got the better of us and turned into an expression of resentment, meaning that they had defrauded us, they'd exploited us, but we were not about to give up, we would not hand anything over, though what it was we wouldn't hand over was not known.

Because who were we dealing with after all, apart from some women with babies in their arms (bleary-eyed driveling Arab babies wrapped in rags and good-luck charms) and a few other women clasping their hands and mumbling as they walked? There were also a few old men walking silently and solemnly as though toward Judgment Day. There were some middle-aged men there, too, who felt they weren't old enough yet to be safe from the impending wrath, and who also felt a need to explain and a rebellious urge that manifested itself from time to time in a look or two. There was a blind man led by a child, perhaps his grandson, who walked along looking around him in bewilderment and curiosity, oblivious to the hand on his shoulder or the trouble hanging over their heads, so that even when he stumbled occasionally he hardly stopped staring at us. And with all these blind, lame, old, and stumbling people, and the women and children all together like some place in the Bible that describes something like this, I don't remember where—in addition to this bit of the Bible, which was already weighing on our hearts, we now reached an open place in which there stood a wide-spreading sycamore tree under which we saw sitting in a huddle the entire population of the village, gathered in silence, a great dappled mass, all collected together, a single silent assembly following what was happening with their eyes, one of them occasionally sighing, "O dear God."

Those whom we had brought along found themselves places of their own accord and gathered under the tree, men and women separately, and sat down heavily, so that at once you could no longer distinguish them from the others. There were many people gathered here, a larger catch than expected, with dark robes and white head-coverings (a scarf wound around a low tarbush for the men and a white embroidered kerchief for the women). Some of them sat swaying to and fro as if they were praying. Others ran their honey-colored amber or plain black worry-beads aimlessly through their fingers. Others folded their big wrinkled peasant arms across their chests, while still others crushed stalks of straw or blades of grass between their fingers just for something to do, and they were all watching us, clinging to our every movement, and not a word did they speak, apart from that occasional sigh, "O dear God."

Among the women, meanwhile, a monotonous, almost incidental weeping started up, which occasionally mounted to a loud sobbing and was choked back. Some women bared a breast to their babies, some covered their faces with a veil, leaving only frightened eyes, some addressed broken phrases and reprimands to their children, whose patience had given out, and who had begun to fidget, approaching us, resting one bare foot upon the opposite knee, and devouring us with their glances, staring wide-eyed at the sight of our every move, as if it were a performance. Only rarely did a single cry burst forth and open the pent-up hearts and tears, and then a general weeping broke from the women, until one of the old men raised his voice and rebuked them, and they gradually controlled themselves.

However, when a stone house exploded with a deafening thunder and a tall column of dust—its roof, visible from where we were, floating peacefully, all spread out, intact, and suddenly splitting and breaking up high in the air and falling in a mass of debris, dust, and a hail of stones—a woman, whose house it apparently was, leapt up, burst into wild howling and started to run in that direction, holding a baby in her arms, while another wretched child who could already stand clutched the hem of her dress, and she screamed, pointed, talked, and choked, and now her friend got up, and another, and an old man stood up too, and other people rose to their feet as she began to run, while the child attached to the hem of her dress was dragged for a moment and stumbled to the ground and bawled, revealing a brown buttock. One of our boys moved forward and shouted at her to stand still. She stifled her words with a desperate shriek, beating her chest with her free hand. She had suddenly understood, it seemed, that it wasn't just about waiting under the sycamore tree to hear what the Jews wanted and then to go home, but that her home and her world had come to a full stop, and everything had turned dark and was collapsing; suddenly she had grasped something inconceivable, terrible, incredible, standing directly before her, real and cruel, body to body, and there was no going back. But the soldier grimaced as though he were tired of listening, and he shouted at her again to sit down with the others. However, the woman was already beyond warnings, she left him behind and started running heavily toward the site of the explosion. With a movement of his hand the boy grabbed her headscarf, and her hair was shamefully disheveled and exposed to view, something that startled everybody and enraged the woman herself. Snatching back her scarf with a wave of rebuke, in a single movement she covered her hair and wrapped up the child, who was bleating with all its tiny might, and hurriedly picked up the hem of her heavy dress and ran toward her ruined home.

"Leave her alone," said someone. "She'll be back."

"*Khawaja*," an old man stood up, apparently one of the most respected men of the village, and came forth from his people toward us, with one hand on his chest and the other extended in front of him in a gesture of courteous request, in a polite manner that both sides would surely recognize as the basis for dialogue, as appropriate to honored interlocutors, and advanced toward us looking among us for someone to open a discussion with. However the one he selected did not let him utter a single word but pointed to where he'd been sitting and said: "Stay in your place until you're called."

The old man started to say something in response, or to rebuke him, thought better of it, shrugged his shoulders, and heavily returned to his place, aided by his cane and the several hands extended to him by those still seated. He sat down heavily and sighed: "*La illah ila Allah*, there is no god but God." Something ancient and biblical once again flickered for a moment, until some other prophecy of doom took its place and hung in the air. Anyone who had forgotten how all this was bound to end knew again what was before him.

"What's this place called anyway?" said Shlomo.

"Khirbet Khizeh," someone answered.

7

IN THE MEANTIME WE WERE CALLED to lunch, and never had a midday break been more welcome. Not just to provide a respite from all that stuff down below, and to enjoy the little warm sunshine that remained of this day and think about other things (and we needed to!), but also, simply, because we were, as could be expected, hungry. Before we got there, Shlomo had already started:

"Its not okay what's going on down there. And there's gonna be more trouble."

"E-nough!" Yehuda squawked like a chicken. "That trash is gonna make trouble for us? No way!"

"I just don't like all this," Shlomo repeated.

"Whatever," said Yehuda. "It's not the movies."

"I just can't stop thinking about those old women sitting there, such fear!"

Since nobody took up the conversation, he continued on his own:

"It was just like the beginning, the first time I saw dead men, wounded men and blood. Do you remember? It was terrible. I thought then that it would haunt me forever. And now, corpses and blood and all that—it doesn't affect me at all."

"You get used to it," Yehuda replied laconically, nodding his head in mock sympathy.

We reached a field off to the side of the houses, next to a wide dirt track that connected this village to the main road, far away. Suddenly, for some reason, a thought crept into my mind, that this track compacted by thousands of feet over the generations would now grow grass, break up, bear fruit with no one passing by. Immediately the chords that had been moaning within me separated themselves, and a wave of bitterness washed through me. And I could sense that troublesome somebody inside me, grinding his teeth and clenching his fists.

We tried to maintain our indifference and shake off everything that had happened down there, like a goose coming out of the water. We distributed the ration tins and the biscuits noisily, with various juicy words, sprawling out on the rotting fallen leaves of a bare fig tree, trying to find something we could laugh about, but underneath it all there was something vague, accumulating in the air, which, despite its brightness, without any connection to what was going on here, had meanwhile become pale and vaguely murky, and white tatters of thickening mists or shimmering water vapor were gathering in the stainless azure, and it was clear that tomorrow or the day after the rain would return.

Shmulik, who was still grieving for his runaway colt, sought to engage Gaby in a very private, very friendly conversation, and said to him, turning his back to us, so as to mark out a separate circle for himself and his friend Gaby, and biting off some of the meat from the tin:

"You don't fancy her?"

"Who?" Gaby hissed dryly.

"Rivkele, you don't think that she's, how should I say, you know, kinda, well, let's just say she's not-like-other-girls."

"She's exactly like other girls," said Gaby.

"No, it's not like that," said Shmulik. "She's kinda proud, don't you think?"

"Not at all," said Gaby. "Or maybe she is, what do I care?"

"You don't care?" said Shmulik in amazement. "I sure would like to get to know her a bit better."

"Just watch out," Aryeh interjected, "that you don't end up the same way with her as you did with the horse."

So there we were all smiling, eating, filling our bellies and passing the time, and we started to relax. If my ears didn't deceive me the word *home* was even mentioned here and there (and your heart within you leapt up then at such a wonderful possibility of a solution and a way out). And when we were peeling oranges and enjoying their flowing juice Gaby quizzed Moishe with his mouth full—what else do we have to do here, and he explained how much better it would be if we finished now and went back and left everything else for others to deal with, and so he added rolling his tongue and grinding his teeth—the gun also needs to be taken care of. But Moishe would have none of it. Moishe said to us as follows:

"First of all, we still have to check all the Arabs assembled below and identify any suspect youths. Second, when the trucks come we'll load them all on and leave the village empty. Third, we have to finish the burning and the demolition. After that we can go home."

My innards clenched for some reason and I was disgusted with the food. I could sense that I was feeling sorry for myself and what awaited me. I don't know what others felt. Impatiently I waited for Gaby to go on grumbling and raisings objections as usual, so that I could get what I wanted as usual, and he didn't waste any time. What, demanded Gaby straightaway, what have we done today and what have the others done today? How far have we walked and how far have they walked? How far have we dragged the machine gun and the ammunition chests and how much have they sat under the sycamore messing around? And he also said that it was about time that we got to go home first for once, people were always taking advantage of us, and so on and so forth—which expressed more and more my own hidden, bursting desire to get up and leave and get out of here quickly before it started to happen for real. Because if it had to be done let others do it. If someone had to get filthy, let others soil their hands. I couldn't. Absolutely not. But immediately another voice started up inside me singing this song: bleeding heart, bleeding heart, bleeding heart. With increasing petulance and a psalm to the beautiful soul that left the dirty work to others, sanctimoniously shutting its eyes, averting them so as to save itself from anything that might upset it, with eyes too pure to behold evil, who has looked upon unbearable iniquity. And I hated the entirety of my being.

However, all Moishe saw fit to do in reply to Gaby's entire discourse was to say with more than laconic brevity:

"That's it."

We gathered our equipment and went down to the makeshift prison by the sycamore tree. After debating with myself I gathered up the courage to say to Moishe:

"Do we really have to expel them? What more can these people do? Who can they hurt? After the young ones have already . . . what's the point . . ."

"Well," Moishe said to me affectionately, "that's what it says in the operational orders."

"But it's not right," I protested, not knowing which of all the arguments and speeches that were fighting within me I should set before him as a decisive proof. And so I simply repeated: "It really isn't right."

"So what do you want?" said Moishe, shrugging his shoulders. He left me. I would have chosen, for various reasons, not all due to moral strength, to remain silent myself, but since I'd started and since Yehuda was walking by my side, I turned to him and said:

"Why do we need to expel them?"

"For sure," said Yehuda, "what are you gonna do with them? Would you assign a company to guard them?"

"What harm could they possibly do?"

"They can, and how. When they start laying mines on the roads, and stealing from the settlements, and spying everywhere—then you'll notice them, and how."

"These people?"

"What do you mean? Are they too small, are they too virtuous? And apart from that there's always going to be two or three or more of them that you won't even know about."

"It's just fantasies," I said.

"So what do you suggest?" said Yehuda.

"I just don't know anymore . . ."

"If you don't know—then shut up," said Yehuda.

And it seemed that this was the advice that I had preferred from the outset. But I was overburdened with words. And once I had started I didn't know how to stop. And since I had no one to argue with—I argued with myself. And this is what I said to myself: But this is a war! Well is it a war or isn't it? And if it's a war, well, all's fair in war. Second voice: War? Against who, these people? First voice (continuing as though he's heard nothing): Perfect saints they're not (but who is?). And even if our intentions are good and honest—you can't go into the water and not get wet (wonder of wonders!). To understand and agree that we've got to act—that's one thing, but to set out and harden your heart and do all sorts of things—that's always something else . . . What's more, who is it who has to be tough and harden his heart? Whoever happens to be tough, and indifferent, anyway. Short break. Immediately, with an apologetic fury that turned into a counterattack: And those villages that we took by storm in the war, were they any different? Or those who ran away of their own accord, frightened by their own shadows? Or villages full of bandits, for whom the fate of Sodom is too good, weren't they entirely different? But not this . . . not this . . . something was still unclear. Just a kind of bad feeling. Like being forced into a nightmare and not being allowed to wake up from it. You're caught up with several voices. You don't know what. Maybe the answer is to stand up and resist? But maybe, the opposite, to see and be and feel until the blood flows in order to . . . in order to what? Time is passing. Time is passing. Man. (Emotional pause.) You are so weak. (Another pause.) If you look you'll burst. (Bleeding heart, bleeding heart, bleeding heart!)

Beneath the sycamore the huddle had grown in the meantime. There were several dozen now sitting in a circle, maybe a hundred people altogether. If you glanced sideways and overlooked the circumstances you could have easily been misled into recalling those village market days, a birthday, the commemoration of some nabi or sheikh, when everyone gathered together in the same kind of huddle, under every green tree, in any puddle of shade, waiting in a festive heaving moving mass, like a lump of dough, not bothering about flies or smells or sweat or the crush and hubbub, so long as that thing, that festive thing they had been looking forward to, happened—but this silence left no room for such delusion, even when now you could hear a sort of buzzing like bees, a furtive rustling, seething, and swelling, in the shade of the great tree. One man, with a prodigious mustache, sat at the edge of the circle patiently rolling a cigarette in his dark peasant hands, transforming the lap of his robe into a tiny workshop for the purpose, gathering up the crumbs of tobacco and packing and tamping them in the trumpet of paper, tapping it this way and that, fussing with his flint and tinder until it finally produced a glow, which was nurtured with blowing and shielded with the cup of a hand, and lit it, raising for his enjoyment a pungent cloud of smoke, demonstrating the last scrap of freedom remaining in his possession, and also some hope for a future, a sort of everything-will-be-all-right that someone always kindled through wishful thinking, which he immediately believed in as though it were the first step toward salvation and even infected his neighbors with his good faith—such a fine quality, which was now made all the more pathetic and gullible since you (like the Lord in Heaven, as it were) knew what he did not know yet.

There was someone else right next to him, and this one was sketching in the sand, slanting, crossing, and winding lines, moving his finger in the paths of the sand with an absentmindedness that was a different form of concentration, but it was not hard to read what he'd drawn, the declaration of a broken man.

What if one of them were to stand up and say, We're not moving from here, villagers, take courage and be men!

My eyes roamed this way and that. I was ill at ease. Where did this sense come from that I was being accused of some crime. And what was it that was beginning to press upon me to look for excuses? My comrades' calm behavior only intensified my own sense of distress. Didn't they realize? Or were they just pretending not to know? They wouldn't even believe me if I told them, apart from the fact that I didn't know what to tell them, and if only I knew how to say what was inside me. I was uneasy. I needed something, something to grasp hold of. I clung to that famous phrase in the operational orders "operatives dispatched on hostile missions." I conjured up before my eyes all the terrible outrages that the Arabs had committed against us. I recited the names of Hebron, Safed, Be'er Tuvia, and Hulda. I seized on necessity, the necessity of the moment, which with the passage of time, when everything was settled, would also be set straight. I once again contemplated the mass of people, seething indistinctly and innocently at my feet—and I found no comfort. I prayed at that moment that something would happen to seize me and take me away from here so I would not see what happened next.

At this very moment Moishe turned to me and told me to get on the jeep with the wireless operator and Shlomo and Yehuda and go check out the area. It was easy to understand how I leapt up and how we uprooted ourselves from where we were (with all eyes watching our actions) on the double, despite the narrow winding lanes. This filthy Khirbet Khizeh. This war. The whole business.

We climbed the slope of a hill, which had never even in its dreams seen anything driving over it with such dizzying boldness, as the incline was dislodged beneath wheels that repeatedly grabbed at its cascading pebbles; drawing a momentary effort, and raging with all its strength and joyful desire at a trial of strength, the jeep quickly reached the topmost height, and there we sought out a place and surveyed the entire land below us.

A first glance and the great land stretched out before you, emphasizing all its sharp-hewn outlines, hunched and hollowed with drenched lushness, in a light that was growing whiter, and with a bit of a breeze that had started in the meantime and blew upon us a breath of beauty, of enjoyment, to the point that it could be tasted, a thrill of pleasure. Everything took on a new dimension, areas were opened and closed, and it appeared there was something that had almost been forgotten but actually seemed solid, and you could lean on it—until the next moment, as its being became real, suddenly here was the checkerboard of fields, plowed and verdant, and the patches of shade-dappled orchards, and the hedges that dissected the area into peaceful forms stretching into the distance, and the variegated hills that blocked and revealed distant pale bluish horizons—and suddenly upon all these an orphaned longing descended, a shadowy veil. Fields that would never be harvested, plantations that would never be irrigated, paths that would become desolate. A sense of destruction and worthlessness. An image of thistles and brambles everywhere, a desolate tawniness, a braying wilderness. And already from those fields accusing eyes peered out at you, that silent accusatory look as of a reproachful animal, staring and following you so there was no refuge.

Then we saw in the distance, on another hill, which was cut by the big dirt track, several trucks rolling heavily along, crawling like blind beetles, struggling with the potholes in the road, their sound still inaudible. Apparently what I was thinking was visible on my face without my knowing it, as the wireless operator, in the midst of his communication, turned to me and said:

"You're in some mood today, what's up?"

"I'm not in any mood today, and nothing's up," I snapped in a tone that didn't exactly suggest the sound of sheep chewing cud at sunset, and that shouted, if you don't mind—"you wanna get hit, come and get hit!" with the vehemence of a man cursing another out of hatred for his face that had betrayed what he held in his heart.

We descended from the hilltop, into the jaws of death (that flattered my inner thoughts), to another plantation, and while we were sinking into the sludge and the mire, frantically moving backward and forward trying to find a way out, Yehuda, who had climbed out to help by pushing, got doused by a dollop of mud and came back to us, smeared, dripping, and sprayed; he bellowed a heartfelt roar at the driver for his witticisms that were no longer funny and cursed our laughter and mockery, promising that he would show us, but his fury still hadn't been assuaged when we finally emerged onto the dirt track, nor even when we comforted him with the thought that as soon as he was dry the whole lot would fall off without leaving a trace, because mud isn't dirt but simply wet soil.

We continued to circle on the desolate paths, we wandered between hedges huddled like frightened sheep, crossing open, spongy, absorbent tracks, beyond which the crops were sprouting as from time immemorial, combed by the breeze with waves of shallow shadows, with their usual ebb and flow. But I imagined I saw a hand inscribing sternly, "Won't be harvested," and wearily crossing the entire field and its neighbor, and passing over the fallow, and the plow, and being swallowed up with a faint shudder among the hills. We examined the entire agricultural plan of the village and its fields, we fathomed their purpose in selecting places for planting, and we grasped their reasoning in the layout of the vegetable plots; the purpose of the field crops, the fallow land, and the crop rotation became clear to us, it was all so evident (even if you could have planned something better suited to our tastes, and we had already started to do so, without realizing it, each of us in his own mind) and all that was needed was for them to come and carry on with what they were doing. Some plots were left fallow, and others were sown, by design, everything was carefully thought out, they had looked at the clouds and observed the wind, and they might also have foreseen drought, flooding, mildew, and even field mice; they had also calculated the implications of rising and falling prices, so that if you were beset by a loss in one sector you'd be saved by a gain in another, and if you lost on grain, the onions might come to the rescue, apart, of course, from the one calculation that they had failed to make, and that was the one that was stalking around, here and now, descending into their spacious fields in order to dispossess them.

Since the paths were muddy, and because we had circled the extremities of the fields (no one had appeared, apart from one time on a hillock to the side, when we saw a few people, but a single shot scattered them as though they had been swallowed up by the earth), we returned to the big dirt track after a considerable delay, and when we drove up onto it, four big transport trucks were waiting there in a row, in front of a long pool of water, which had opted for idleness and fallen peacefully asleep in the middle of the road, without leaving any room to pass on either side, and on its shores the drivers and their assistants were standing around, roaring advice and warnings to the other side, and apart from some other expressions they also said they had had enough of sinking in—and from now on the hell with it. It wouldn't—in their view—hurt any Ayrab in the world to stir his dainty feet and walk up here, and thank us for this too! Meanwhile, facing them was our lieutenant who roared at them from the other side, but it was clear that he wasn't making any headway, and, in fact, he was losing ground, his claim that you didn't sink to the bottom of standing water was not accepted by anyone, since they refused to believe in the existence of any bottom underneath the water. Then our jeep was chosen to be the guinea pig and they suggested that we should cross the water, both fast enough not to get stuck and slowly enough not to get stuck. Of course exactly in the middle of the puddle, for some reason, our engine stalled, and it hardly mattered that a moment later it started up again and the jeep crossed the pool as easily as anything, spewing turbid waves on either side, apart from a filthy jet that found its way to the last remaining dry spot on Yehuda's clothing, and the poor wretch was so enraged that he could only maintain an ominous and ludicrous silence, but the matter was not settled and the drivers refused to listen and declared that they were turning round, in various maneuvers, on the spot, on the dirt track, and we should bring our Arabs up through a gap in the hedge, and we had wasted so much time for nothing, which was exactly what they had predicted at the outset. Then our lieutenant climbed back into the jeep and returned to the village, leaving us with instructions to widen the gap and prepare the way.

Naturally none of us lifted a finger, apart from casually bashing two or three cactus leaves with our rifle butts, and instead we sat down to watch the struggles of the drivers with their clumsy vehicles in the narrow road, appraising each of their movements with professional knowledge, artistic insight, and cigarette smoke. But Yehuda went to the other side, the sunny one, and stood there casting disappointed glances at the sun and wondering at its power. In the midst of all this activity, we did not notice the sudden arrival of the first groups of Arabs, who stood before us with that distinctive smell of their clothes. At once our laughter died down and we put on curious, dutiful faces, and I had the impression that we felt that something was beginning here, something that was greater than what we'd been expecting, apparently.

I don't know if they had been told before they left what was awaiting them or where they were being taken. At any rate their appearance and their gait recalled nothing so much as a confused, obedient, groaning flock of sheep, unable to take stock of their situation. Nevertheless, here and there, a few of them appeared to be imagining the worst, and some of them may have even been suspecting, wordlessly, with fear in their hearts, with panic in their breasts, that they were all being led to the slaughter.

The first group was standing by the gap in the hedge. This field might have belonged to one of them. And this place, which we considered just any old place, they considered a specific place that was close to something and far from something else and belonged to somebody and had a greater meaning than just some big dirt track. They stared at the trucks with a gaze that gradually filled with a realization of what was happening to them. And then they turned their eyes on us, seeking out among us someone with whom they might be able to speak, from whom they could hope for something. One of them, in a striped robe with a gleaming buckle on his leather belt, held up his left hand, with the bent fingers of a working man who was not working, and grumbled something. Immediately someone shouted at him in a voice that, whatever it was like really, sounded unnecessarily loud and grating: "*Yallah! Yallah!*" And the anonymous mass of people started moving and stooped at the breach, and came through one after another, and they continued walking uphill in a row along the low cactus hedge, and came out again on the other side of the puddle next to the first truck, whose tailgate had been lowered.

The driver and his mate stood there to keep them moving, extending a hand to one or another and sending him on his way with a push, saying a word to one, observing about this one that he was fat and about that one that he must be a real bastard, and about yet another that he was so old he must be eighty or even ninety, for sure. It was amazing how none of them protested or objected. With resignation they climbed up and huddled together on the truck.

"That's it," said the driver with satisfaction.

"Count how many you've got there," they shouted at him from this side of the water.

"How come they're not taking any stuff with them?" asked the driver.

"What stuff?" they asked him.

"Possessions, bedding, I dunno."

"There's no stuff. There's nothing. Take them away from here and let them go to hell," they answered him from our side. And again there was something that didn't seem right or proper, but nobody interfered.

At this point suddenly from on top of the truck an Arab, the one with the striped shirt and shiny belt buckle, turned to us and said:

"*Ya khawaja*"—his voice gaining strength as he spoke—"*ya khawajat*," he corrected himself to the plural "sirs," so as to address us all, and he started speaking, reciting, expounding, as though he were reading holy writ, and with something of the vehemence of someone who knew he was innocent and could prove it. But we couldn't understand much of what he was saying, and the harsh guttural consonants of his pronunciation seemed strange and almost exaggerated to us, like sounds in and of themselves. Our silence only encouraged him and he waved his left hand to reinforce his demands, and there seemed to be a rustle of approval from on board the truck and glances from there watching for any sign of success. But in the meantime the next group had begun approaching, and we stopped paying attention to him.

The new arrivals moved in line. The sight of their predecessors on the truck startled them and they stopped walking. There were some women at the end of the line, and a sound of weeping broke from them. (My skin began to tingle.) It seemed as though this time something would happen. Two old men passed in front of me, mumbling as they walked, both to each other and each to himself. They tried to pause opposite the jeep, which seemed to them a place of honor, to have their say, but they were waved on with *yallah yallah*. And they did what they were told. But instead of crossing at the gap in the hedge they continued straight through the puddle, their bare feet dabbling in the water as they casually raised the hems of their robes, as if there was nothing special about walking through a puddle, and the others walked behind them, assuming that this was the way, splashing through the water. Somebody sighed and removed his shoes to walk through the water. I don't know why this gesture seemed so humiliating and demeaning. Like animals, I thought, like animals. However, as soon as the women had crossed one of them turned toward us and took hold of Shlomo's sleeve, weeping and pleading with him. Shlomo shook her off, looking here and there for suggestions, or, maybe, permission to show her pity. But Yehuda, who was standing there, forgetting all about his spattered clothes, said to her sternly: "*Yallah yallah*, you too!" And the woman, startled, walked on, while Shlomo said dismissively, either by way of explanation or excuse: "And what would she have done all alone in the village anyway . . ."

Then a woman came toward us clutching a skinny baby, lugging it like an unwanted object. A gray-hued, gaunt, sickly, undersized infant. Her mother held her in her rags and waved and danced her in front of us as she said to us with something that was neither mockery nor disgust, and not crazed weeping, but, perhaps, all three together: "Do you want her? Take her, take her and keep her!" We screwed up our faces in revulsion, and seeing this, she apparently took it as a sign of success and continued to dangle the pitiful creature, bound in filthy rags, in one hand, while with the other she pounded her chest, "Here, take her, give her bread, take her and keep her!" Until someone thought better and said to her sternly, *Yallah, yallah* and even raised his hand—I don't know why—and she fled, half-laughing half-weeping, and entered the puddle, dancing the baby in her hands, laughing and weeping brokenly.

"They're just like animals!" Yehuda explained to us, but we did not reply.

The women were gathered onto another truck, and they began to scream and weep, and no one envied those who had to look after them. And there was one guy by the truck, who raised his voice and shouted at them that they had nothing to cry for because we weren't going to do anything to them, just take them to their husbands. But whether it was his Arabic or his reasoning that was not understood, the screaming and weeping only intensified, and they fell upon him since he had given them an opening, with a thousand cries, demands, complaints, accusations, entreaties, and pleas, until he retreated in confusion, and somebody else put him out of his misery by silencing them with the full blast of his voice.

Next some more people went past saying nothing and not looking at us, and their appearance made us feel like worthless idlers and mischievous hoodlums. Then a cripple passed by digging little holes in the wet sand with his wooden leg. He smiled at us apologetically for some reason, and hopped into the puddle, when a fleeting thought suggested that he should really have been asked to go round it or that he should simply be left behind. A short, stocky man passed, and when he reached us he tried to shout, breathing heavily and sucking up his saliva, either to spit it at us or to make room to shout, but he made do with vigorous gestures intended to explain, to threaten, to demand or ask, then sighed deeply, sighed again, and went on his way. Next came four blind men each holding the shoulder of the one in front, and groping with a stick in their free hand, their eye sockets turned slightly upward and more to the side than was necessary, as though their ears were going first, and over and above the special attentiveness that blind people have and a fear of stumbling at the next step, they suffered from a great and general fear that came from not knowing anything about where they were going or what there was in the place they were going to or what the others were doing. So they groped their way along (it was amazing how they had managed to find one another and form a group), and when they reached the puddle, somebody came to them and took the hand of the first one, who nodded his sparsely bearded head toward him, straining his senses even more intensely, and said: *Uq'adu hon*—sit here. And they turned back to the embankment of the road and sprawled where they had stood, wondering what this was all about. They seated an old man who was bent double beside them. We felt a mood of beggary, pus, and leprosy, and all that was lacking was the sound of dirges and *charity saveth from death.*

"Ugh, revolting!" said Shlomo.

"Better they should die!" said Yehuda.

"How many blind people and cripples do they have in this village!" said Shlomo.

"The others fled, and they left them here for us," said Yehuda. "But now the rope will follow the bucket, and they'll return to their owners."

"But why do we have to deal with all this?" burst from my mouth, with greater vehemence than I had expected.

"Right," Shlomo agreed. "I'd rather have ten battles than this business!"

"What's the matter with you!" grumbled Yehuda, scratching at the layers of solidified mud with his fingernails. "What are we doing to them? Are we killing them? We're taking them to their side. Let them sit there and wait. It's very decent of us. There's no other place in the world where they'd have been treated as well as this. Anyway, no one asked them to start with us." He paused for a moment and on reflection added: "What'll happen to them over there? Let them ask their beloved leaders. What will they eat or drink? They should have thought of that before they started all this!"

"Started what?" I said.

"Don't you make yourself out to be a saint!" Yehuda said furiously. "Now at last we've established some order in these parts!"

But Shlomo continued as he'd begun: "When you go to a place where you might die that's one thing, but when you go to a place where other people are liable to die and you just stand and watch them, that's something quite different. At least that's what I think."

"You're another one!" shouted Yehuda. "Stop thinking so much. And if that's the way you feel, you can go with them, where they're going. If that's the way you feel!"

"Don't shout at me!" shouted Shlomo. "And I'm not asking you where I should go," he said and walked away from us.

"So excitable!" Yehuda said to the world in general rather than to any one person in particular. "I'd like to see *them*, with Arabs conquering *them*, in *their* village, where *they* live!"

"That's just why," I started to say.

"What do you mean that's just why, nobody asked them to start these wars and things. Such great saints. Too much of our own blood has been spilled because of them! Those nothings! Let them eat what they've cooked!"

Then we saw a woman who was walking in a group of three or four other women. She was holding the hand of a child about seven years old. There was something special about her. She seemed stern, self-controlled, austere in her sorrow. Tears, which hardly seemed to be her own, rolled down her cheeks. And the child too was sobbing a kind of stiff-lipped "what-have-you-done-to-us." It suddenly seemed as if she were the only one who knew exactly what was happening. So much so that I felt ashamed in her presence and lowered my eyes. It was as though there were an outcry in their gait, a kind of sullen accusation: Damn you. We also saw that she was too proud to pay us the least attention. We understood that she was a lioness, and we saw that the lines of her face had hardened with furrows of self-restraint and a determination to endure her suffering with courage, and how now, when her world had fallen into ruins, she did not want to break down before us. Exalted in their pain and sorrow above our—wicked—existence they went on their way and we could also see how something was happening in the heart of the boy, something that, when he grew up, could only become a viper inside him, that same thing that was now the weeping of a helpless child.

Something struck me like lightning. All at once everything seemed to mean something different, more precisely: exile. This was exile. This was what exile was like. This was what exile looked like.

I couldn't stay where I was. The place itself couldn't bear me. I went round to the other side. There the blind people were sitting. I hastily skirted round them. I went through the gap into the field that was bounded by the cactus hedge. Things were piling up inside me.

I had never been in the Diaspora—I said to myself—I had never known what it was like . . . but people had spoken to me, told me, taught me, and repeatedly recited to me, from every direction, in books and newspapers, everywhere: exile. They had played on all my nerves. Our nation's protest to the world: exile! It had entered me, apparently, with my mother's milk. What, in fact, had we perpetrated here today?

There was nowhere to wander or to distance myself. I went down and mingled with them like someone looking for something.

Words rang in my ears. I did not know where from. I passed among them all, among those weeping aloud, among those silently grinding their teeth, those feeling sorry for themselves and for what they were leaving behind, those who railed at their destiny and those who quietly submitted to it, those ashamed of themselves and their disgrace, those already making plans to sort themselves out somehow, those weeping for the fields that would be desolate, and those silenced by exhaustion, eaten away by hunger and fear. I wanted to discover if among all these people there was a single Jeremiah mourning and burning, forging a mouth of fury in his heart, crying out in stifled tones to the old God in Heaven, atop the trucks of exile . . .

The puddle on the road was in the shade now, and passing ripples on its surface subsided to caress the reflection of the sky. I sought an explanation for the tremors running through me, and where this echo had come from, an echo of tramping feet ringing in my ears, an echo of the feet of other exiles, dim, distant, almost mythical, but wrathful, like a jeremiad, rolling like thunder, distant and menacing, a harbinger of gloom, beyond which, an echo carrying dread—I couldn't bear it any longer . . .

8

I BUMPED INTO MOISHE.

"What are you looking at me like that for?" said Moishe.

"This is a filthy war," I said to him in a choked voice.

"*Dahilak*, please," said Moishe. "So what do you want?"

And there was something I really did want. I had something I wanted to say. I just didn't know how to say anything that would be practical wisdom rather than merely emotion. Somehow I had to shake him. Quickly and immediately I had to bring him face-to-face with the seriousness of the situation.

Instead of which Moishe pushed his cap back away from his forehead, like someone exhausted from too much work, like a man talking to his friend, scrabbling in his pockets after cigarettes and matches and trying to clothe in words something that had just occurred to him, and answered me:

"Just you listen to what I'm saying." Moishe's eyes sought mine as he spoke. "Immigrants of ours will come to this Khirbet what's-its-name, you hear me, and they'll take this land and work it and it'll be beautiful here!"

Of course. Absolutely. Why hadn't I realized it from the outset? Our very own Khirbet Khizeh. Questions of housing, and problems of absorption. And hooray, we'd house and absorb—and how! We'd open a cooperative store, establish a school, maybe even a synagogue. There would be political parties here. They'd debate all sorts of things. They would plow fields, and sow, and reap, and do great things. Long live Hebrew Khizeh! Who, then, would ever imagine that once there had been some Khirbet Khizeh that we emptied out and took for ourselves. We came, we shot, we burned; we blew up, expelled, drove out, and sent into exile.

What in God's name were we doing in this place!

My eyes darted to and fro and couldn't fix on anything. Behind me the village was already beginning to fall silent, its houses gathered on the slope of the hill, bounded here and there with treetops, from which the sun, behind them, forged silent shadows, which were sunk in contemplation, knowing much more than we did and surveying the silence of the village, that same silence which, more and more, was conspiring to create an atmosphere of its own, a realization of abandonment, an oppressive grief of separation, of an empty home, a deserted shore, wave upon wave, and a bare horizon. And that same strange silence as though of a corpse.

And why not? It was nothing. A single day of discomfort and then *our people* would strike root here for many years. Like a tree planted by streams of water. Yes. On the other hand, what of the wicked ... But they were already there on the trucks, and soon they'd be nothing more than a page that had been finished and turned. Certainly, wasn't it our right? Hadn't we conquered it today?

I felt that I was on the verge of slipping. I managed to pull myself together. My guts cried out. Colonizers, they shouted. Lies, my guts shouted. Khirbet Khizeh is not ours. The Spandau gun never gave us any rights. Oh, my guts screamed. What hadn't they told us about refugees. Everything, everything was for the refugees, their welfare, their rescue ... our refugees, naturally. Those we were driving out—that was a totally different matter. Wait. Two thousand years of exile. The whole story. Jews being killed. Europe. We were the masters now.

The people who would live in this village—wouldn't the walls cry out in their ears? Those sights, screams that were screamed and that were not screamed, the confused innocence of dazed sheep, the submissiveness of the weak, and their heroism, that unique heroism of the weak who didn't know what to do and were unable to do anything, the silenced weak—would the new settlers not sense that the air here was heavy with shades, voices, and stares?

I wanted to do something. I knew I wouldn't cry out. Why the devil was I the only one here who was getting excited? From what clay was I formed? This time I'd become entangled. There was something in me that wanted to rebel, something destructive, heretical, something that felt like cursing everything. Who could I speak to? Who would listen? They would just laugh at me. I felt a terrifying collapse inside me. I had a single, set idea, like a hammered nail, that I could never be reconciled to anything, so long as the tears of a weeping child still glistened as he walked along with his mother, who furiously fought back her soundless tears, on his way into exile, bearing with him a roar of injustice and such a scream that—it was impossible that no one in the world would gather that scream in when the moment came—and then I said to Moishe: "We have no right, Moishe, to kick them out of here!" I didn't want my voice to tremble.

And Moishe said to me: "You're starting with that again!"

And I realized that nothing would come of it.

It seemed such a shame, such a crying shame.

The first transport had already moved off without my noticing and was climbing the big dirt track. (If only I could go from one to the next and whisper to them, come back, come back tonight, we're leaving here tonight and the village will be empty. Come back! Don't leave the village empty!) At once the second transport moved off too, the one with the women, who decorated the truck with the blue of their dresses and the white of their headscarves, and a single wail rose aloft, and was inserted into the sobbing of the heavy truck that grated and grabbed its way in the wet sand. (And the blind men would surely be forgotten here by the roadside.) It was the afternoon. Against the tranquillity of the sky leapt the anger of the wind that darkened the day and foretold new rain, tomorrow or the day after. Here and there in the village there rose a trail of white smoke from damp materials that refused to burn, and refused to go out, and would go on smoking like this, half-burning, for a few days, until suddenly a wall or roof would collapse. A cow bellowed somewhere.

When they reached their place of exile night would already have fallen. Their clothing would be their only bedding. Fine. What could be done? The third truck began to rumble. Had some astrologer already seen in the conjuncture of the stars in the sky over the village or in some horoscope how things would turn out here? And what indifference there was in us, as if we had never been anything but peddlers of exile, and our hearts had coarsened in the process. But this was not the point either.

And how does it end?

The valley was calm. Somebody started talking about supper. Far away on the dirt track, close to what appeared to be its end, a distant, darkening, swaying truck, in the manner of heavy trucks laden with fruit or produce or something, was gradually being swallowed up. Tomorrow, both painful humiliation and helpless rage would turn into a kind of casual irritation, shameful but fading fast. Everything was suddenly so open. So big, so very big. And we had all become so small and insignificant. Soon a time would arise in the world when it would be good to come home from work, to return exhausted, to meet someone, or walk alone, to walk saying nothing. All around silence was falling, and very soon it would close upon the last circle. And when silence had closed in on everything and no man disturbed the stillness, which yearned noiselessly for what was beyond silence—then God would come forth and descend to roam the valley, and see whether all was according to the cry that had reached him.

May 1949

AFTERWORD:
BACK TO KHIRBET KHIZEH

Khirbet Khizeh is a canonical text, a masterpiece of modern Hebrew prose and, in theory, still an optional part of the standard curriculum in Israeli high schools. I used to think this was a fine thing. I thought it meant that even official Israel—the Ministry of Education!— had the confidence and courage to look at itself in the mirror. After all, the image isn't very pleasant. S. Yizhar (his real name was Yizhar Smilansky) was the first major writer to describe in credible, unforgettable detail one emblematic example of the expulsion of Palestinian villagers from their homes by Israeli soldiers, acting under orders, in the last months of the 1948–49 war. The story, for all its complexity, cuts right through the prevalent nationalist myth that, like all nationalist myths, blames everything unpalatable on the ever-available "enemy." Isn't that what enemies are for? But here is a case where the Establishment seemed to make room for a dissonant, destabilizing voice, something in the tradition of the Hebrew prophets—the voice of conscience. Yizhar was an intelligence officer in the Israeli army in 1948; he wrote about what he himself had seen and felt. Unfortunately, it's not at all clear that young Israelis who read this tale of what is, for them, a very distant past are likely to connect it in any meaningful way to their lives today. There is a mystery here, one very close to Yizhar's own eloquent depiction of the interplay of insight, willful blindness, and straightforward confusion in the consciousness of his unhappy characters.

I first read the story over forty years ago, in Iowa, when I was an ungainly adolescent drunk on the Hebrew language and eager to move to the one place in the world where this language was fully alive. I remember being struck and deeply disturbed by the work, but I didn't really understand it. Such are the ironies of my life that I finished rereading it last week in a Palestinian village called Twaneh, in the south Hebron hills. Here is one more Yizhar-like tale—that of a Jewish boy who comes to live in Israel, who revels in the light and the smells and the tastes of the ravishing landscape, who goes to war (a foolish, needless war, in Lebanon in 1982), who gradually wakes up and eventually finds his way to Twaneh to stand with the villagers, along with other like-minded Israelis, against their common foes, the Jewish settlers intent on terrorizing these people and driving them off their land. It isn't a pretty story.

Twaneh, spilling over a thorny hilltop, is a village of radiant charm, intensified perhaps by the sense of precariousness that shadows every moment there. Last Saturday was a day of pristine, early-winter sunlight, rather like the one in *Khirbet Khizeh*. Every crack and fissure, every shrub and pebble, each house of rough-hewn stone stood out, starkly contoured, on the brown sweep of the hill. Most of us have powerful memories from this place; I will never forget the rainy day the settlers shot at us and beat us when we came to guard the villagers as they plowed their field. This time we sat, sipping tea, in the sun at the entrance to Hafez's house as we rehearsed the possible scenarios for next week's action—a solidarity march to Tuba, just over the hill. The night before, settlers from the "outpost" of Havat Maon attacked the villagers yet again; three villagers were arrested by the police on trumped-up charges along with one of the international volunteers stationed in Twaneh. We heard the story from dignified, unfailingly cheerful Ali, our friend from Tuba; his children walk the footpath each day to their school in Twaneh, braving the threat from Havat Maon; his daughter was badly wounded in the eye in an attack some two years ago. It is that same path that we'll walk next weekend with the volunteers. While waiting to leave, as the sun slid toward the horizon, I stole a few moments to finish reading the story that has gripped me for days, that seemed as close to me as the walls and hedges and stones of the village. I think I understand it now.

I had forgotten the tough, supple feel of Yizhar's Hebrew (splendidly translated here by Nicholas de Lange and Yaacob Dweck). No other Hebrew prose is remotely like it. Today it's a vanished language, this experimental mélange of wild, lucid lyricism, often dark and menacing, pointed biblical allusions that go off like hand grenades in the midst of the meandering, stream-of-consciousness syntax, and the bizarre, somewhat stiff colloquial speech of his tormented protagonists. Modern Hebrew was much younger then, sixty years ago, but haunted, of course, like everything written in this language, by the grisly and compelling ghosts of the distant past. Look at a simple sentence like the following: *zik ha-tzayyadim ha-omem be-khol adam nitlake'ah banu atah bi-gvurah*, "The thrill of the hunt that lurks inside every man had taken firm hold of us." This comes at an early moment in the story, when the narrator and his comrades, still far outside the village, are just beginning to strafe it with their machine gun. "Thrill" translates the Hebrew *zik*, which means "a spark" (also perhaps a firebrand and a comet or shooting star), and the word immediately calls up for the Hebrew reader passages like Proverbs 26:18–19, which speaks of the man who, *pretending to be mad*, shoots "sparks, arrows, and death" (*ha-yoreh zikim hizim va-mavet*) in order to delude his neighbor. Feigned, lethal madness masking deceitful malice—it's easy to see how the verses feed into Yizhar's dense web of allusion. And we have Isaiah 50:11, threatening the enemies of the Lord who will, says the prophet, eventually walk into the "burning fire and the firebrands" they have ignited (*uve-zikot bi'artem*). And so on. It's not enough that these soldiers are happily shooting at innocents, or that the thrill they feel is recognized at once as something universal, hidden inside every man; the very words conjure up the sinister and the sinful. And the sentence ends on a still more bitter and ironic note, for "taken firm hold of us" is *bi-gvurah*—the standard Hebrew term for "in strength" or "with heroism." The sordid thrill has *heroically* taken hold. Our young heroes are already enmeshed in incipient crime. (And I have still not said anything about the astonishing, possibly unique, tragic adjective *omem*, translated here as "lurks inside," and conveying darkness, obtuseness, or a failing of light.)

Yizhar's text is saturated with such tones. No sentence is innocent, no matter how preoccupied it may seem to be with the physical beauty of the fields, the sky, the season, or some other apparently extraneous perception. (Yizhar is perhaps the greatest poet of Palestinian landscape in modern Hebrew.) The narrator takes in the sensual world around him, it fills his eyes and penetrates all his pores, at moments it seems to offer a desperately sought distraction, yet the intense beauty of this world ultimately intensifies an experience of emergent human evil. The contrast itself can hardly be contained. The infuriating incongruity of extreme natural beauty and overwhelming pain inflicted by others, with or without obvious intention, is something all Israeli peace workers know well.

A little farther into the story, as the first houses are being blown up and their owners cower in shock and fear:

> We had a sudden sense of foreboding as though we were about to be attacked, the alien walls were closing in on us, encompassing us with solemn malicious whispering, suddenly we seemed cut off, devoid of hope, no one knew whence the blow might suddenly fall— unless there were no other—and we ourselves were it, in our image and likeness.

Again the culmination devastates the reader: the slightly scrambled syntax, so characteristic of Yizhar, produces sudden insight (the horror is not external to the narrator and his companions) and then the inevitable biblical and/or liturgical resonance. "In our image and likeness" is *bi-dmutenu ke-tzalmenu*: a tormenting echo of Genesis 1:26–27, or, if you prefer, of Genesis 5:3 or Psalms 39:7 or the most exquisite of the seven blessings spoken under the Jewish wedding canopy, the one that affirms that human love is the direct result of our being created *be-tzelem dmut tavnito*, "in the very image of God's own form."

The most famous of all such linguistic infiltrations comes in the final word of the story: *ha-ke-tza'akatah*. This is Genesis 18:20–21: "Verily, the cry of Sodom and Gomorrah is great, and verily their sin is exceeding grievous. I will go down now, and see whether they have done altogether according to the cry of it *[ha-ke-tza'akatah]*, which is come unto Me." Here is Yizhar's reworking: "And when silence had closed in on everything and no man disturbed the stillness, which yearned noiselessly for what was beyond silence—then God would come forth and descend to roam the valley, and see whether all was according to the cry that had reached him." The Hebrew sentence ends with the dangling phrase—"according to the cry"—and this is all the reader needs to conjure up the image of a moral and social depravity so unredeemed that it can only call down destruction. The heavy silence the narrator imagines in fact shudders with a wordless scream. All of this is in that one last unmistakable word that leaves the story open-ended, wounded, incapable of ever coming to rest.

It is easier, it seems, to talk about the language than about the themes of this story; I've been putting off this moment. The trouble is that, in parts, it's so painfully familiar. Khirbet Khizeh could easily be any of the dozen or so Palestinian villages that I've come to know over the last few years, working the peace front on the grassroots level inside the occupied territories. Same stone houses, same twisting lanes, same random assortment of donkeys and camels and horses and chickens, same vineyards and olive groves and fields, same succulent language, same clothes, same faces—often sad and scared. And there are the obvious differences, too. The story was published in May 1949. Things happen in war. Sometimes we say this to ourselves, as a kind of mantra, meant to comfort. War is war, right? The expulsion of large Palestinian populations, along with the flight of many others, was part of the wider context; the new state had been attacked by Arab armies, it was a life-and-death struggle; these are things we know, things taught in the schools. Maybe they help some Israelis tell a story that makes sense to them. "Nobody asked them to start these wars and things," says Yehuda toward the end of the novella. "Let them eat what they've cooked!" I've heard those words, and others like them, hollow and self-serving, too many times. Anything to even the score, as if it could ever be evened, as if some perverse calculus of right and wrong could produce an equation that helped *our* side come out ahead in the final reckoning.

Today things take a different form—though for a Palestinian experiencing daily life in the occupied territories, or for someone like me who has become a certain kind of witness to that life, Yizhar's trenchant text has uncanny relevance. If you happen to live in Twaneh or Susya or Tuba or any of a hundred other villages, the threat of expulsion is very real. It is generally much slower in pace than the sudden cruelties of 1948. There is also some hope that we can stop it, using whatever means we have at our disposal—the media, the courts (although their record is abysmal when it comes to the territories), our physical presence on the ground, our words, yes, even words may be of use. Meanwhile, the everyday reality is grim. Palestinian Susya—thirteen families still clinging to the last small piece of their historic lands on a hilltop across from the Israeli settlement of Susya—has demolition orders hanging over all of its meager huts and tents. The Susya villagers have already been deported four or five times—forced by soldiers and, it seems, their settler-allies into trucks in the middle of the night and dumped on the road many miles away (shades of Yizhar). Each time they have come back to what is left of their homes. The vast machinery of the Israeli system of occupation—the military courts, the bureaucracy, the committee (dominated by settlers) that issues, or rather declines to issue, building permits, the politicians, the soldiers stationed in south Hebron—all this is brought to bear on this one tiny spot, as if the mere presence of these Palestinian survivors is intolerable to those who have taken their land. At Twaneh, settlers spread poison in the Palestinian fields, hoping to wipe out the herds of sheep and goats on which the villagers subsist—hoping to force them to leave. At Tuba, which has the singular misfortune of having Havat Maon for its neighbor, sheer physical survival is a daily challenge. Tuba is cut off from any road, utterly isolated, its people subject to constant depredations; the whole area of the village and its lands, like much of the south Hebron hills, is included in a sweeping order of expropriation meant, ostensibly, to turn this region into what is known in Hebrew as a "firing zone," that is, a training area for the army. The possibility of exile looms before them. The Supreme Court has not yet pronounced on this case.

In short, and sad to say, what began in 1948 under different circumstances continues today, and there is at the moment no war to provide even the semblance of a rationalization. All Israelis know this, though most pay no attention. What happens to the people on the "other side," as it is called, is of little consequence. And yet, in some ways our situation is perhaps after all a little better than that described in Yizhar's story.

Notice, for example, the fact that the narrator, for all his revulsion at what is happening, never even considers refusing to carry out the order. Of course, most soldiers would never resist, though a faint hint of the idea does pass through the narrator's mind:

> But not this . . . not this . . . something was still unclear. Just a kind of bad feeling. Like being forced into a nightmare and not being allowed to wake up from it. You're caught up with

several voices. You don't know what. Maybe
the answer is to stand up and resist? But
maybe, the opposite, to see and be and feel . . .

To refuse is not a serious option here. One can't
help identifying with this speaker, who allows himself
to feel, who won't surrender to the anesthesia that
normally comes into play in such situations; who won't
look away. And he is not entirely alone. The soldiers at
Khirbet Khizeh are certainly not demonic figures. They
are ordinary people, frightened and exhausted, caught
up in an overdetermined, violent conflict and in evil
that takes on many forms. It isn't all their fault, though
they are party to a crime. They have doubts; some of
them can almost imagine their victims' pain. Here is
Shlomo, drawing the inevitable conclusion: "When you
go to a place where you might die that's one thing, but
when you go to a place where other people are liable to
die and you just stand and watch them, that's something
quite different. At least that's what I think." To which
Yehuda characteristically replies: "Stop thinking so
much."

It's a common enough solution. But in Israel
today, literally thousands of young Israelis have refused
to serve in the army of occupation. Many quietly make

arrangements with their units and their officers; many hundreds have gone to jail for their act of conscience. A few have demanded, on principle, to be tried at a full-scale court-martial—a huge risk, since it carries with it the possibility of three years' imprisonment. They want to look the army in the eye and force it to acknowledge its complicity in the evils of the occupation. Despite everything, there is ample space for such acts of principle. In my very first week in the Israeli army, in 1977, one day before we were to swear our oath of allegiance and obedience unto death, an officer from the General Staff in Tel Aviv was sent to talk to us, to explain the meaning of the oath. Someone asked him what we should do if faced with an order that we regarded as immoral. To his immense credit, he answered: "There is no rule for such a situation. It is between you and your conscience." I'm not sure today's recruits would hear such an answer. I'm not sure they wouldn't. But for a soldier who refuses today, the deep loneliness that Yizhar's hero describes is perhaps a little less severe.

Sometimes even the helpless villagers are not quite so alone. In 2002, settlers from Itamar and Tapuach—two of the most predatory Israeli settlements in Samaria—drove the inhabitants of Kafr Yanun from their village. The Palestinians were ready to give up, unable to stand the daily routine of terror and humiliation, ready to go into exile. Israeli activists from Ta'ayush—"Arab-Jewish Partnership," one of the most effective of the peace groups—brought them back to the village and stayed with them for weeks to protect them from the settlers and the soldiers. Kafr Yanun is still there. The lives of its people are far from easy, but they are still there.

In the genealogy of Israeli self-awareness, Yizhar's novella has a niche of its own. Never has the tale been so clearly told. Though there have been attempts to discredit the author, even to brand him (or the film made of his story that was, after considerable controversy, broadcast on Israeli television in early 1978) as treasonous, the story has found its own hidden channels into minds and hearts—not, perhaps, those of the so-called mainstream but rather those situated on the rather more interesting margins of Israeli culture. A direct line links *Khirbet Khizeh* with today's peace movements, peopled by ordinary human beings who will not, under any circumstances, lend their hands to blatant injustice. None of us could formulate the matter with Yizhar's unflinching forcefulness, but there is not one of us who would fail to recognize the feelings he describes—the outrage, the terrible confusion, the grief, the sense of collective self-betrayal, the isolation from one's friends and fellows, the paralysis and hesitation, the bodily urge to protest. "My guts cried out. Colonizers, they shouted. Lies, my guts shouted. Khirbet Khizeh is not ours." All of us have witnessed many times what Yizhar calls "that unique heroism of the weak who didn't know what to do and were unable to do anything, the silenced weak." All of us have experienced the narrator's despair and imitated his final act of sorrow: "There was nowhere to wander or to distance myself. I went down and mingled with them like someone looking for something." He is describing something each of us knows intimately. We are still looking.

It comes down, I suppose, to the instrumental use of human beings and to the creation of a system, driven by greed, that puts such naked instrumentalism before any other value. You'll forgive, I hope, this abstract statement; Yizhar said it better. Malice, like simple decency, has its own irreducible integrity. But perhaps it is worth stressing, by way of conclusion, that this story is in fact far from being moralistic, utterly remote from preaching and pontification. The protest it describes, like the protests enacted by today's activists, comes from another place, somewhere deep inside the body, a site of inadvertent revulsion and unresolved struggle. No one should ever idealize it, no more than Yizhar does in his subtle portrait of the soldier-narrator's quandary. He knew of what he wrote, knew the cost and the fear and the inevitable failure and the murkiness of the moments in which a person might make a choice—even with respect to the rather basic question of what one allows oneself to see. Morality, in the usual sense of the word, is perhaps the least of it. Rather, the choice has something to do with extricating oneself from the thick envelope of one's tribe and neighbors and colleagues, and the words that fill all the open spaces, so as to touch, at least in passing, that elusive, unsentimental freedom that defines the human being. It is from this point that one can act. I believe this is the true import of Yizhar's great text.

So next Shabbat I'll be back in Twaneh together with some two hundred activists, Israeli and Palestinian. We're in it together. (That's another interesting change from 1948.) If the army doesn't stop us, and probably even if it does, we'll march up the stony path to Tuba to ensure that the villagers can plow their fields, this year, in the face of the settlers who will be doing whatever they can to prevent this. These settlers are not about to go away, not yet, and in Tuba one lives a day at a time. Each plowed field is a small victory. Every day that the children of the village arrive safely at their school in Twaneh without being beaten by the settlers en route is a celebration. Maybe we'll briefly change the balance of power, maybe the story of Tuba will find its way into the press, maybe someone will care. We'll be carrying signs, in Hebrew and Arabic, for the benefit of the villagers and the soldiers and the press, signs that say something like "Lift the Siege on Tuba!" and "Evacuate the Settler Outposts" and "No to Occupation, Yes to Peace." Maybe I'll make one for myself: "No More Khirbet Khizehs."

David Shulman
Jerusalem, November 2007

A NOTE ABOUT THE AUTHOR

S. Yizhar was the pen name of Yizhar Smilansky, born in Rehovot in 1916. A longtime member of the Knesset, he is most famous as the author of *Khirbet Khizeh* and of the untranslated magnum opus *Days of Ziklag*. He died in 2006.

A NOTE ABOUT THE TRANSLATORS

Nicholas de Lange, a professor emeritus of Hebrew and Jewish studies at Cambridge University, has translated many Hebrew novels, including *Preliminaries* by S. Yizhar.

Yaacob Dweck translated Haim Sabato's *The Dawning of the Day*. He is an assistant professor of history and Judaic studies at Princeton University.

A NOTE ABOUT THE AFTERWORD AUTHOR

David Shulman teaches Sanskrit and other Indian languages at the Hebrew University of Jerusalem. He has published numerous books and is the author of *Dark Hope: Working for Peace in Israel and Palestine*. Shulman was named a MacArthur Fellow in 1987.